JUST

KNOCK

THREE

TIMES

JUST KNOCK THREE TIMES

ROSE D. BENTLEY

Halo
PUBLISHING
INTERNATIONAL

Halo Publishing International
7550 WIH-10 #800, PMB 2069,
San Antonio, TX 78229

First Edition, September 2023
ISBN: 978-1-63765-464-4
Library of Congress Control Number: 2023914039

The information contained within this book is strictly for informational purposes. Unless otherwise indicated, all the names, characters, businesses, places, events and incidents in this book are either the product of the author's imagination or used in a fictitious manner. Any resemblance to actual persons, living or dead, or actual events is purely coincidental.

Halo Publishing International is a self-publishing company that publishes adult fiction and non-fiction, children's literature, self-help, spiritual, and faith-based books. We continually strive to help authors reach their publishing goals and provide many different services that help them do so. We do not publish books that are deemed to be politically, religiously, or socially disrespectful, or books that are sexually provocative, including erotica. Halo reserves the right to refuse publication of any manuscript if it is deemed not to be in line with our principles. Do you have a book idea you would like us to consider publishing? Please visit www.halopublishing.com for more information.

For Allie and Bekki, my best babes
who have always supported me.

PROLOGUE

MYLES

I like to think our decisions in life bring us to where we are supposed to be. For a while, I wasn't so sure about mine. I left the girl I loved when I was barely eighteen—years later, she is still the only woman I have ever loved. At the time, I had no idea that my decision would mean losing her forever.

She was dealt some rough cards in life; my leaving was one of them. She's the kind of girl you don't get over. Her skin is soft and delicate, and her hair feels like silk. Her eyes draw you in deeper than any ocean depth, and her poetic words make you want to stay. She's loyal, loves hard, and would sacrifice her own happiness just for you. If you're lucky, you end up with her. If you're a fool, you lose her.

I understand why she ran away. Her life was consumed with pain, abandonment, abuse, and fear. She once told me I was the only light in her world. Her words play on repeat in my mind, *"Myles, you have always been the light in my dark world."*

I believed her.

I've always been told that feelings are neither good nor bad. They just live with us, and it is up to us whether we learn how to reside with them or let them take control of us. She was the kind of girl who learned how to live with it. Her interior was tough, but in a silent way. Unfortunately, her exterior, in a terrible way, was often covered in bruises and wounds.

I begged her to let me help, but the fear of separation consumed both of us. I admit it made me feel less of a man, but I was also still just a child.

The first time we spoke was in fifth grade. She had lost control, and I felt the need to jump in and help her. Once I did, I never wanted to stop. I was eleven, and in my head, I played movies in which I was a superhero; she was my damsel in distress.

Sometimes I'd watch her from my backyard, which her bedroom overlooked. She was an artist, and when she was painting, she'd get lost in her work. She never even once noticed that I was staring at her.

In the summers, her cheeks were freckled, and the strawberry strands in her hair got lighter. In the winters, her skin grew paler, like a stunning piece of porcelain.

I knew when she was sad; she wore it like a heavy winter coat. I also knew when she was happy because she'd share that delight with *me*. I studied her every moment I got, and to this day, I'm not sure if she noticed just how much I adored her.

Love wasn't in question; that was obvious. Is there something even deeper than unconditional love? If so, that is what would explain my feelings toward her.

She was sublime, and at one point, she was mine.

CHAPTER ONE

PENELOPE

I sat on the toilet seat in the girls' bathroom at my elementary school, tears streaming down my cheeks. It took everything in me to not leave this stall and go smack Piper Evans clear across the face.

My mom left three years ago. She just disappeared one morning and never came back. Sometimes I'm angry about it; other times I'm heartbroken. I don't understand how a mother could leave her daughter the way she left me. No explanation, just gone.

I used to cry myself to sleep when I thought about how much fun we had. She'd take me into the forest and dance barefoot with me. Our matching blush-blonde hair swayed with our steps. We made bracelets out of skinny twigs and decorated them with smeared green moss. We enjoyed finding pieces of nature and using them to the best of our creative abilities.

At bedtime she sang me old lullabies, similar to the ones Viking women sang to their babies. Earthy and strong-hearted songs, but she sang them so delicately as she rubbed my eyebrows and watched me fall asleep.

Her skin was always so warm; she was everything to me. It was just she and I for a while. I don't know who my dad is; he might not even know I exist, for all I know. But, whoever he is, he missed out. My mom was beautiful and graceful, and our lives were pure bliss.

This was true up until we went to live with my grandparents. She sat me down one day and told me that we needed to move on to our next chapter and that our purpose in that home had been fulfilled. "We are going to go live with Grandma and Grandpa," she told me while we were packing. "You don't need much, baby. Just bring some clothes and toys."

One morning we woke up before the sun was even awake. The house seemed different that day; it was gloomy and sad. As if it had just lost its only family.

I held my favorite teddy bear in my arms and jumped into the front seat of our 1970 boxwood-green Ford Bronco. We drove away, leaving our perfect little house on the rural roads of Coupeville, Washington.

I loved that home. It was painted a light blue and had vines growing on the sides. We only had two bedrooms, but it was spacious and had big windows. Our backyard was so green, and on the hill behind us was a miniature rainforest.

Mom and I had painted a mural in my room, a flower garden with every color you could think of. She was a painter; she painted murals for people in their houses. One of her customers paid her enough to finance our trip to Southern California once. We spent a week on the beach in San Diego; it was the best week of my life.

To get to my grandparents' house, we had to take a ferry across the bay. I remember Mom and I getting out of the car and watching the ocean over the rail. We took any opportunity to be near any form of nature.

My grandparents live in a town called Port Townsend. It's coastal, kind of like Coupeville, and it's mostly known for its Victorian buildings. Main Street is kind of cool too, but it's a tourist trap. Frank and Hollie Wolfe were owners of a yellow, two-story house with a big backyard. It was centered in the heart of a residential area, not rural, as was the home we just abandoned.

Mom and I shared a room, which I loved. We also started a flower garden in a perfect spot in the backyard. We pretended it was a flower shop and named it Iris and Penny's Fabulous Flowers. Penny, short for Penelope.

Every morning before school, we picked fresh flowers from our garden and put them in a glass jar on the windowsill of our bedroom. At night, after the picked flowers wilted, we took them to the backyard and laid them next to the planted flowers, so they could become part of the earth again.

Iris Wolfe, my mother, whom I adored with every bone of my body, left three months after we moved. All she took were some of her clothes.

Piper Evans used to be my friend before my mom left. Then, shortly after she told me that something was wrong with me—"*Why else would a mother leave?*"—and she didn't want to be around me anymore. She chose a Friday, before the start of Mrs. Oden's homeroom class, to taunt me in front of everyone.

"Smelly Penelope is so smelly, just like her ugly shoes," she chants. "Smelly Penelope is so smelly she has to wear flowers in her hair to hide the odor."

I did wear flowers in my hair, but it wasn't because I stank. I kept Iris and Penny's Fabulous Flowers alive and picked a fresh flower every morning, I placed it in my hair and wore it until it got dry and weak. It reminded me of my mom.

I think Piper's jealous of me. She has no other reason to hate me.

We take the same art class, and Mr. Fry, our art teacher, has always been impressed with my work. In fact, three of my pieces have been put on display in our classroom so far this year.

Piper is always talking about how she's going to be a famous artist someday. If she doesn't outgrow her mediocre work, I don't see that happening.

"Smelly Penelope is so smelly her mom had to leave her behind just to get away from the stench."

That's the one that got to me. I grabbed my backpack, stormed out of Mrs. Oden's class, and went straight into the bathroom. Filled with anger, I cried. *Why is she such a bitch? Why can't she just leave me alone?*

Five minutes goes by before Mrs. Oden comes into the bathroom, looking for me. "Penny?" she says softly.

I ignore her.

"Penny, it's me, Mrs. Oden...just me," she says.

I suppose I can't stay here forever.

I slowly open the stall. My face is puffy, and my eyes are swollen.

"Oh, honey," she says as she gives me a gentle hug. "I'm so sorry."

Mrs. Oden is aware of my absent-mother situation; she is in the same book club as my grandma. When Grandma hosts the book meeting, Mrs. Oden comes over, always makes sure to say hi to me, and checks out how my flower garden is doing.

I hug her back, but say nothing.

We stand there for a while before she speaks again. "Penny, we need to get back to class. I talked to Piper and told her what she is doing is unacceptable. She has a meeting after class with the principal."

I nod and accept that Mrs. Oden can't stand in this bathroom with me all day.

"I'll meet you in class," she says and leaves the bathroom.

I look in the mirror; my green eyes are always greener when I cry. Also, I'm a spitting image of my mother. I return to the class as slowly as I can and take a seat in the back.

Mrs. Oden gives me a reassuring smile, but Piper makes sure to scowl at me as if I were the one who did something wrong.

When class ends, I try to rush through the hallway to avoid Piper.

But she catches up. "Thanks a lot, Penny. You got me in trouble." She grabs my arm.

"How did I get you in trouble? You're being a jerk!" I say loudly and pull my arm back.

"You're just always so grumpy," she says then lets me go. She starts to walk ahead of me, but stops and turns around and taunts, "Is it because your mom left you?"

What happens next is out of my control. I black out. My vision turns red. I can't breathe or think straight in that moment. I grab Piper by the back of her frizzy brown hair and pull her to the ground. I sit on top of her and slap her across the face while tears rush down mine. I couldn't stop even if I wanted to.

"You're such an asshole, Piper!" I scream. "I hate you!"

Someone grabs my waist and pulls me off her.

"No!" I yell. "I hate you!"

"You're going to get in trouble," they say and keep pulling me farther away. "Come on; let's go."

Luckily, no adults have seen what happened, but I'm sure Ms. Prissy Piper is on her way to tell on me. Part of me feels bad about reacting that way, but another part of me feels good about it.

Piper went too far, and if I hadn't defended myself, she would have continued to bully me throughout the rest of our school years. I hate her.

"Are you okay?" he asks.

I had forgotten that I was escorted outside by someone. It turns out it was Myles Ford, my neighbor.

Myles lives next door to me with his mom, dad, and little brother. His family has lived there since before he was born. They seem to be so happy. I often see them barbecuing on Sundays, giggling, and throwing a football around. Sometimes they have a backyard bonfire and cook up some s'mores. I like the smell of the campfire; I can smell it from my bedroom window, which overlooks their backyard. Sometimes I pretend that I am sitting with them and involved in their conversations. I eavesdrop and laugh silently in my bedroom at Mr. Ford's dad jokes.

His mom gardens too, but she plants mostly vegetables that she harvests and cooks. They are so tasty. I only know this because sometimes she brings over leftovers. Grandpa hates vegetables, so Grandma and I get to enjoy them.

Washington is the *best* state for gardens and greenery. The rainfall and humidity are plants' best friends.

"I think so," I say to Myles, coming back to reality.

"She's stupid." He smiles and playfully nudges my side.

I smile and respond, "Yeah, she's stupid."

"I'll walk you home," he says and turns in the direction of our block.

School had just started for the day, but there was no way I could walk back in there. Myles didn't seem to mind leaving either, and Grandma and Grandpa said that they were going to be out for most of the day. So I guess we were playing hooky.

Neither of us says anything on our walk. I keep thinking of how much trouble I am going to be in once my grandparents found out. I think Myles can feel my anxiety, so he probably doesn't want to upset me more than I already am.

It's about a thirty-minute walk home, and the only car in the driveway is my mom's Bronco. She must have gotten a ride from someone when she left because it's been sitting in the same spot for three years. Its loneliness proves that no one is home.

Myles walks me to my front door and asks, "Do you want to hang out?"

I haven't really spent any time with Myles, outside of the occasional banter between his family and my grandparents in passing, but I like the idea of not being alone right now.

I nod and say, "Do you want to come in? I have some board games." I'm embarrassed that I don't have anything cooler than Candy Land and Connect Four.

"I like games!" he says excitedly.

I get the spare key from under the mat and unlock the door. Our house is dreary, and everything is brown. The wallpaper is starting to peel, and it has an odd smell. Our living room, dining room, kitchen, and a bathroom are downstairs, while the three bedrooms and other bathroom are upstairs. One of the rooms is used for storage; it's so packed it looks as if a hoarder lives in there. I try not to think of how nice Myles's house probably is, compared to mine, and hope he's not creeped out by the unwelcomeness of where I live.

I get Candy Land from the shelf in the dining room and bring it into the kitchen where Myles is waiting. "Are you thirsty?" I ask him, hoping he only asks for water.

Tap water and microwavable food are the delicacies of the Wolfe residence—except for book-club nights. Grandma will usually cook up something when the ladies are coming over.

"No, thanks, I have a water bottle in my backpack," he says while sitting at the kitchen table and opening the game box. "Ready to lose?" He smirks.

"You mean are YOU ready to lose," I respond and giggle.

Four hours go by quicker than I thought because I'm startled to hear the front door open. Myles and I look at each other wide-eyed.

"Oh no," I whisper, "you need to hide."

Before he has a chance to respond, I open the door to the bathroom and push him inside of it. "Hide in the shower," I say and close the door. I rush back to the kitchen table just in time for my grandpa to see me.

"You're home early," he says with concern.

"Uh, yeah, I wasn't feeling well," I lie.

"You little fucking lying bitch," he yells, instantly going from concerned to livid. "I just got a call from your principal. He said you got into a fight and then ditched school," he shouts and walks towards me. He grabs me by the shoulders and shakes me. "What in the hell were you thinking?!"

I smell alcohol on his breath. I look to my grandma to see her reaction, but she just looks at me sadly and walks up the stairs.

He takes one hand off my shoulder and uses it to backhand me. "You want to fight someone? Huh? Well, here you go." He hits me again with so much force that it knocks both me and my chair to the floor. I start to cry and feel blood oozing from my upper cheek.

"You are not to leave this house except for school. Do you hear me, young lady?!" he screams in my face. Bits of his saliva fall onto my nose. "And if you misbehave again, you're going to wish you were dead." He spits at my feet and wobbles over to the stairs. "Fucking eleven-year-old kid fighting at school. I'll show her a fight," he mumbles as he ascends.

I wipe my face with the sleeve of my shirt, trying to remove both the tears and saliva. This isn't the first time Grandpa has hit me. It only happens when he's drunk and if I have done something to upset him. He seems to be upset about a lot of things though.

Grandpa is someone I am afraid of; I wouldn't dare stand up to him the way I did to Piper today. I don't want him to kick me out, or drive me somewhere far away and leave me there for dead. I don't like him one bit, but he and Grandma are the only family I have.

The worst beating was when I went to look for my mom a couple of weeks after she left. I didn't tell my grandparents where I was going, I just ran out the front door. I looked everywhere my legs could take me. Grandpa found me down by the harbor, looking inside of docked boats.

That night, I suffered bruises on my ribs, a black eye, and a bloody nose. I remember lying on the floor as his foot struck my abdomen and eventually my face.

Grandma stays quiet mostly. She tends my wounds though. She cleans off the blood and applies some anti-bacterial ointment and then gauze or a Band-Aid. But now that I am eleven, I can take care of it myself, so she usually hides in their bedroom.

It suddenly occurs to me that Myles is still in the bathroom. I quickly get up, forgetting about the blood on my face.

"Myles, I'm so sorry," I say as soon as I open the door.

He jumps out shaking. "Are you okay?!" He immediately grabs me and pulls me in for a hug. "I was going to jump out and fight him, but" —he gets quiet for a second and pulls away—"I got scared," he admits.

For a moment, I don't feel the pain in my face, only the comfort of the hug. It's the second one today, which is two more than I've had in about three years.

Myles's bright-blue eyes look down to the floor.

I hear rustling upstairs. "You better go before he sees you," I say and nudge Myles toward the back door. "You can go out back and through the side gate," I whisper.

"Wait, Penny! Should we call the cops? Or tell my parents?" he whispers loudly.

"No, please don't," I beg.

He steps outside the back door, but before he leaves, he says, "I'm scared for you."

"I'll be okay. Please don't tell," I repeat as I quietly close the door. I place my back against it and slide down to the floor. *What a day*, I think to myself.

Once I have myself gathered, I go into the bathroom and clean my wound; it's mostly dry now, but I don't want to get an infection. So I clean it up with some hydrogen peroxide and stick a Band-Aid over it. When I'm done, I clean up the game and make myself some mac 'n' cheese, my favorite comfort food.

Sometime later, I hear a tiny tapping sound at the back door. I set the bowl down on the kitchen counter and tiptoe over to it. Grandpa has been snoring for over ten minutes, but I don't want to make a peep. I'd hate to be the one who wakes him up when he's trying to sleep off his drunken state.

When I open the back door, I see a letter and plate of cookies on the step.

Penny,

I can't stop feeling bad about what happened with your grandpa. I didn't tell my parents, but I did ask my mom if we could make some cookies. Her cookies make everything better, so I thought maybe they'd help you.

Myles

PS—Meet me at your side gate tomorrow at 10 AM.

My heart warms a little. Myles has been through this entire day with me and still is interested in being my friend. I look around, but there's no sight of him. So I pick up the plate, quietly run upstairs, snuggle up on my bed, and devour every last crumb.

He was right; they did make me feel better.

Chapter Two

Myles and I have spent every possible second together since the day he witnessed me take down Piper. He has become my best friend.

Almost the entire summer after fifth grade, I taught him how to garden.

"Should we plant sunflowers?" he asked me one morning when we were digging up dirt.

"Sunflowers are pretty, but not as beautiful as daffodils," I said to him, smiling. I was in my element—dirt under my fingernails and a cup full of seeds.

He was so excited come spring to see what would grow out of the little spot in his backyard. To his delight, they were perfect, and he told me I was his lucky charm.

In sixth grade, we walked to and from school every day together, minus the winter months and the week that I had the flu. That whole week, he brought me end-less amounts of his mom's chocolate chip cookies, and we wrote letters back and forth.

Myles,

Today was terrible. I haven't stopped throwing up. The only thing I can eat are those delicious cookies. I was able to do a really cool painting too. I painted a picture of some butterflies and bees. It's kind of small, but I hung it up over my bed. I really like it.

Anyways, tell me what happened at school!

Penny

He wrote back:

P,

You didn't miss much, except it rained, so we had PE inside, and a fight broke out between Justin and Whalen today. That was cool.

I'd love to see your painting; maybe you can bring it out to show me. Bees are awesome. Aren't they? I know most people are scared of them, but I'm not.

Can't wait until you feel better!

—M

Justin and Whalen Simpkins are identical twins, and they are always fighting. So it didn't surprise me that they had a tussle in PE. Plus, they both like the same girl—Lacey Mower—who happens to be my friend too.

Myles and I haven't talked much about what happened that day when he was hiding in the bathroom. Or when it happens in general. He knows when Grandpa hurts me because I try to hide any marks or bruises and don't do a very good job at it. He'll ask questions sometimes; other times, he just hugs me. I think it's become kind of the norm for us, sadly.

One of my teachers saw a mark on my arm once and called Child Protective Services. A tall lady with straight black hair and wearing a blue suit came to our house and interviewed us. First Grandpa and Grandma, then me.

"Penelope, does your grandma or grandpa hurt you?" she asked me with a pen in one hand and a clipboard in the other.

"No," I responded.

"How did you get those bruises on your arm?"

"I play outside a lot, and I'm pretty clumsy."

"Mm-hmm, okay. Well, just so you know, if someone ever did hurt you, we have people who can help and safe places that you can go to," she told me after taking off her glasses and looking directly into my eyes.

"Okay, thank you." I couldn't look back into her eyes because I felt as if she could see right through me.

I guess they didn't have enough evidence to remove me from my grandparents' care without my admitting to any abuse. Which I was grateful for. As much as I hated this house and my grandpa, I didn't want to leave. Piper Evans was finally leaving me alone, I had an amazing garden in my backyard, I had started to master my painting skills, and I had Myles. I didn't want to end up with some strangers who wanted me to call them family. For all I knew, it could be worse than it was here.

The summer before seventh grade, I started developing breasts, and sometimes I'd catch Myles looking at me differently. He still acted the same for the most part though.

There was a time we went to John Wayne Marina on a school field trip at the end of May, right before school ended. The marina was in Sequim, Washington, and it was only about an hour's drive from our school.

There was a small beach area in the marina where you could hang out. We all brought sack lunches and laid our towels on the sand.

Myles was sitting with Justin, while Lacey and I were putting our feet in the water. She suggested that we go in completely. Even though the water was chilly, I happily agreed. I loved the water. However, I remember the beaches in San Diego were much warmer than any of them here.

We took off our shorts and tank tops, revealing our swimsuits underneath. I caught Myles staring at me. I must admit, I made sure my posture was ideal. I peeked back a few times here and there and noticed he never took his eyes off me.

Lacey was clueless, still childlike; she just wanted to swim around and splash me. My distraction because of Myles's looking at me drifted away with the waves, and I joined her in the fun. I felt as if half of my child-hood bliss was stripped away when my mother left, and the other half was gone the first time my grandpa decided to hit me. So moments when I was able to feel like a kid meant the world to me.

Lacey was one of my friends, and I really liked spending time with her, but Myles was my most treasured person on this whole planet. Sometimes I felt as if he had filled the hole my mother left in my heart. Well, he and my art.

I've acquired a lot of supplies from the throw-out pile at school. If the bottle is covered in paint, or if the tube is half empty, they throw it away. So I've taken that opportunity to grow my art-supply collection.

When I'm not with Myles, I'm painting or molding something out of clay. I have a pretty big stack of art piled up in my closet. Some nights when I can't sleep, I'll sit in there with a flashlight that I stole from the junk drawer in the garage and reminisce.

I like to paint things that I remember. Like my old house in Coupeville. I tried to recreate it perfectly, but it doesn't feel completely accurate, which bothers me. Maybe one day I can go back there and paint it in person.

I started my period shortly after that beach trip. I was terrified. They had taught us about puberty in sixth grade, but it was just a twenty-five-minute video with cheesy actors. Lacey started hers before me and told me how it felt. So I kind of knew what to expect, but it didn't take away the panic that came with it.

I sat on the toilet, watching the blood drip out of me. There were no pads or tampons stored in the bathroom, so I just wadded up some toilet paper and stuffed it in the bottom of my underwear.

This is something that a mother should be here for. I guess my next-best option is Grandma.

I told her the next day about starting my period. She went to the store and bought me what seemed like a whole year's supply of necessities.

"Do you know what to do?" she asked when she was placing them in the back of the bathroom cupboard.

"Yeah, kind of."

That was the extent of the conversation.

On the first day of eighth grade, my grandma died. It happened in her sleep; she had a brain aneurism. The medical personnel who came and inspected her said she likely didn't feel any pain, and then they took her away in an ambulance.

Having the paramedics in my home was kind of exciting to me. I liked it when people were in the house; it took away some of the dreary loneliness.

One of the paramedics even commented on my painting that I had stuck on my bedroom door. "Did you paint that?" he asked.

"Yeah, I did," I said, happy that he'd noticed.

"It's beautiful." He smiled back at me and continued to help his partner carry the stretcher downstairs.

I'm not sure if that was his way of comforting a girl who had just lost her grandmother, or if he genuinely liked it. Either way, it brought a little warmth to my heart.

Grandpa didn't seem sad, just angry that he had to plan a funeral for Grandma. Anger seemed to be his choice of feeling, unfortunately.

I was upset that she died. I didn't look up to her and wasn't very close to her, but we did have a couple of good memories. Outside of her tending to my wounds from one of Grandpa's lashings, she'd watch movies with me on the weekends. Sometimes she'd take me with her to the grocery store and let me pick out a sweet treat. She would pick one too, and we'd sit in the market's parking lot, eating them. She had my mother's eyes too. I liked looking at her and remembering Mom.

We had a funeral for her at their church; it's ironic that a man like Frank Wolfe attended such a holy place. Everyone from her book club came, including Mrs. Oden. Some ladies from her favorite restaurant were there, along with some other neighbors and the Fords.

As I walked, I scanned the faces of everyone. I was thinking that maybe my mom had heard that Grandma died and that she would show up. I'm not sure why

I expected that, but I was so disappointed when she never did.

I wore a black wrap dress that my mother had left behind. It had a fading maroon-paisley pattern. It was a little too long for me, but it would do. Grandpa didn't like spending money on me, so most of my clothes were from what my mom had left and from Lacey. She'd developed sooner than I and was a little taller, so I took the things she had outgrown. To finish off my outfit, I plucked a light-purple coneflower from my garden and wore it in my naturally wavy, blonde hair.

Lacey had no idea what my home life was like. She just thought that we were poor, so she was always happy to give me her old clothes. Her mom worked for a clothing store, so she was always bringing Lacey new things to wear. I ended up getting some really cute stuff. Grandpa never asked where they came from; I think he was just glad that he didn't have to deal with it.

Myles sat next to me on the church pew. Grandpa insisted on sitting in front; luckily, so did the Fords. Myles's mom often exchanged books with my grandmother, so they were somewhat close, but not close enough to know that when Grandpa drank, he would sometimes beat Grandma too. Which is probably why she kept quiet all those times he was beating on me.

When it was Grandpa's turn to deliver a eulogy for his late wife, he stood up and slowly made his way to the podium that stood in front of her casket. "Thank you, everyone, for coming. My name is F-F-Frank, and Hollie was my w-w-wife. I must say she was a good wife..." He went on about how they met, then were married shortly after. He mentioned the birth of my mom too. I felt exhausted by the time he was finally done; he'd slurred his words through the whole thing.

Myles squeezed my hand when he noticed the slurring. His gesture was a message. It told me he was sorry, and he was there for whatever came next. I noticed his other hand's clenched fist.

Myles was taller now and a little more filled out. Sometimes I wondered if he could take Grandpa, but the bigger part of me thought Grandpa would separate us and deny my seeing Myles if something such as that were to ever happen. I think we both had that fear. I believe that was the only thing stopping Myles from waltzing into the house and hitting Grandpa with a baseball bat.

After the funeral, I saw Myles's parents, Steve and Victoria, talking to Grandpa. Probably giving their condolences and likely noticing, too, he was drunk. To my surprise, they all walked to where I was waiting.

"Penelope, would you like to come with us to grab an ice-cream cone?" Victoria asked me.

I looked at Grandpa, seeking some form of approval, which he gave with a nod of his head. "I'd love to," I responded, smiling.

Grandpa wobbled off to his truck as the Fords and I gathered in their white SUV and made our way to the Sweet Spot, a local ice-cream place.

I had the best time. Steve and Vicky—she insisted that I call them that—were very attentive to me. They asked a lot of questions about my art, what kind of TV shows I watched, and if I had any other hobbies. Myles and his little brother, Aaron, were play fighting and trying to dunk each other's faces in their ice creams.

Is this what a happy family looks like? Feels like? I'd kill to have my mom here with me—or even a dad, for that matter.

I wished so badly to go home with the Fords, cuddle up on their sofa, and watch their nightly TV sitcom together. I wanted to wake up to the smell of pancakes and bacon and hear the faint sound of jazzy music playing. I wanted to play fight with Aaron and chase him around the breakfast table with a runny egg. Then, after breakfast, I'd go dig up more dirt with Myles.

Instead, I had to go home. *Home* is such a strong word with so many different meanings.

When we got back to our neighborhood, I thanked them for their time and generosity, and gave Myles a smile before walking into my house. Grandpa was on the couch, watching something on the History Channel; I tried to immediately go to my room, but he stopped me.

"Penny, where the fuck have you been?" he asked angrily.

"Grandpa, I was with the neighbors getting ice cream, remember?" I reminded him, scared that he'd already forgotten. I noticed multiple empty beer cans on the coffee table.

"I don't know what you're talking about, but you know the rules. You come straight home!" he yelled and stood up.

"Grandpa, you can ask Vicky and Steve; you said it was okay!"

Before I could plead more, he was standing right in front of me with a stone-cold face. The next thing I knew, I was face down at the bottom of the stairs. My head was throbbing, and it hurt to open my eyes. I put my shaking hand up to my head and felt the warmth of fresh blood. I sat up slowly and saw a blurry vision of Grandpa on the couch, snoring.

What happened? I asked myself.

It took a few minutes before my mind could make sense of anything. My pain was transforming into rage. I got up and ran out the back door, crying. I sat next to my garden and held my knees, cradling myself like a small child, rocking back and forth. I tried to sob silently, but the cries bellowed out of me as if from a hurt fawn in the middle of a forest.

I heard the side gate open a couple of minutes later and saw Myles running towards me. "Penny, what happened?" he asked, inspecting my head.

"He was drunk and angry and forgot that he had said it was okay for me to go with you guys." I sobbed.

"That's it; we need to call the cops," he said, standing confidently.

"NO. They'll take me away. I'll be put into foster care. I want to stay here," I said sternly.

He sat back down next to me with the realization of what would happen if the authorities did find out.

"I just need to make it to eighteen."

He grabbed my hand and placed his other one over it. "I'm so sorry. I hate him so much."

I felt the anger brewing inside of him. He'd expressed before how badly he hated what was happening to me; sometimes he'd even cried with me.

I laid my head on his shoulder. A little while later, my sobbing stopped, and my heart rate returned to a normal rhythm. We sat there in silence for what felt like an hour.

"You should go in," I finally told him, standing up and wiping the dirt from my dress.

"Will you be okay?" he asked, standing with me.

"Yeah." I tried to smile.

"Listen, if you need to get away, or if you need any-thing—and I mean anything—you tap on my window, okay?" he said, making sure I heard him. "Just knock three times."

CHAPTER THREE

I have been learning how to drive, Myles has been teaching me. Neither of us has our license yet, but his dad taught him over the summer last year.

He was given a 1990 Chevrolet Silverado, blue with a white stripe, for his sixteenth birthday. He LOVES that truck. I'm lucky he's even trusting me in the driver's seat.

"Okay, to start the car, you have to push in the clutch and turn it on. Then let's put it into first gear."

I follow his instructions and push in the clutch and turn on the car. The car starts; the rumble of the exhaust excites me. The idea of knowing how to drive excites me even more.

"Let's put it into gear. Grab this" —he points to the gearshift—"then push it to the left and then upwards; that's first gear."

I continue to follow his instructions.

"Okay, now you have to feather the gas while slowly releasing the clutch to get going."

I do as he says, but I release the clutch too fast, and the car stalls out.

He laughs, and I laugh with him. "Don't worry; you'll get it," he reassures me. "Let's try again."

Grandpa has been supportive of my driving, only because he doesn't want to have to drive me anywhere. When it's too cold, rainy, or snowy, I can't walk to school. Sometimes I catch a ride with Myles, but other times Grandpa has to take me. He couldn't care less if I have to walk in cold or wet weather, but after that CPS visit, he's a little more cautious about getting caught.

He hates it enough that he has to get up and take me to school sometimes, but he would hate it even more to have to teach me. It would take away from his time of hanging out at the bar with his creepy friends, which he has been frequenting much more now that Grandma is gone.

"Have that boy fix up that Bronco out there; you can take that piece of junk," Grandpa told me one morning, nodding towards my mom's old car.

When he told me that I would be getting the Bronco, I was so happy that I almost jumped up and hugged him. Not even Grandpa's shielding himself from my hug would take away the excitement and happiness that I felt.

I don't know much about his upbringing, but it couldn't have been good, being the way that he is. Sometimes I find comfort in reminding myself that he was once a young boy, probably abused at the hands of his own father. He doesn't know any better and is parenting through his own traumas. Not that that's any excuse for laying your hands on someone so violently, but it could explain some of his antics.

I'm so glad to have the Bronco, and I'm even happier that I can ask Myles for help. He and I, still inseparable, are starting to grow feelings. At least, I think he is. I know I am. We haven't talked about it or acted on it, but we both try to find ways to be alone.

Sometimes at school he is with his friends in the lunchroom, but when he sees me nearby, he comes over to sit with me. I usually sit with Lacey and Julianne, a new high school friend, but if I see Myles making his way towards me, I'll scoot a little farther from them so he and I can sit closer together.

There were a few times over the last couple of years that I had it pretty bad from Grandpa. I accidentally spilled some paint on our kitchen tablecloth and couldn't find a cleaning solution that would get it all out. He saw the mess and lost it. He ransacked my room, found my paintings in the closet, and threw them all into the fireplace.

I burned my hand trying to take them out. Grandpa just sat back and laughed at me, taunting me. He told me that it was just trash anyways and would never pay the bills. So why waste my time?

All of that hard work burned to ashes. They were my escape plan. I was going to try to sell them to tourists so I could save up some money just in case I needed to get out of here quickly. I was almost as devastated as I was when my mom left. My art has become pieces of her and memories that weren't stained with pain.

That night I snuck out and tiptoed to Myles's house. I gently knocked on his window, and a few minutes later he was out in his backyard with me. There was a wooden bench near the flower bed.

"I can't wait to be an adult and get out of here," I told him. "I want to go find my mom and tell her what a terrible person she was for leaving me with him."

I have confided in Myles a few times about my mom. He is always sympathetic, but he can't completely grasp my feelings. His mom is sunshine, and he is so lucky to have her, which he is aware of. He is always the sweetest to his mother.

"Where would you go to look?" he asked, kicking at a rock that was embedded in the grass.

"I feel like she would have gone somewhere sunny, like to California," I responded, remembering my trip to San Diego.

"Hmm," Myles said, looking solemn.

"What's up?" I asked him, noticing his change in demeanor.

"Well, I always thought you would just be here. I hadn't realized what will happen when we grow up. Like, what comes after that? We move away and get jobs and find someone to marry and relive what our parents have lived?" he asked, still messing with the rock.

It's true; I hadn't thought of a life without Myles either, or anything past that. The idea of Myles going off and getting married caused a stabbing feeling in my stomach. I regretted saying I couldn't wait to leave.

"Well, maybe I can sell enough art pieces to get us both out of here." I playfully nudged him, trying to keep the idea of our staying together alive.

I didn't mention that Grandpa had burned all of my art. I didn't think the conversation needed another negative aspect to it, but if I was going to try raise some money to get out of here, I had to restart my whole collection.

We spent most of the night talking about what we wanted to do in our lives. He told me he wanted to become a firefighter. "All the girls love firefighters," he joked, but then got serious when he said it was one of the most heroic things he'd seen and that he wanted to be part of something that meaningful.

I dreamed of owning my own art studio where I could create beautiful things and teach others my skill.

"Where do you see your art studio being?"

"Not far from here." I winked. "I'd love to be back in Coupeville."

Eventually it got to be almost dawn and close to the time his dad would be waking up for work. We went our separate ways, but not before he said, "You're an amazing artist, Penny. There is no doubt that you will be able to live out your dream, and I sincerely hope that it isn't too far from here."

On Myles's sixteenth birthday, he asked if I would paint that bench in the backyard for him. "Make it something you'd want to look at every day," he told me.

I didn't have much money, so he knew I couldn't get him a gift. When he suggested that I paint something for him, I jumped on the idea. His mom even let me use some of her supplies. I sanded the bench and stained it a light-gray color. I proceeded to paint all the flowers

Myles and I had planted over the years. Tulips, daffodils, yarrows, purple loosestrife, and so many more.

When I gave the bench back to him, he grinned from ear to ear. "Thank you, this is the best present I got this year," he told me as we put it back in its spot.

"It's even better than the truck?" I asked jokingly.

"Yes, better than the truck." He smiled.

Now, it's almost *my* sixteenth birthday, and I know exactly what to ask from Myles. His dad is a mechanic, so he knows mostly everything you need to know about cars.

"Hey, my grandpa said I could have my mom's Bronco. Is there any chance you'd want to help me fix it up?" I asked him one day on our way home from school.

His face lit up. "Hell yeah! Let's get it going!" He pumped his hand in the air as if he had just won something.

The following weekend we spent every second of daylight with that Bronco. The battery was dead, so we had to get a new one. Steve was happy to help with that. Most of the hoses were clogged and corroded too, which Myles was able to either clean out or replace with fresh hoses.

I couldn't help but watch Myles when he worked. He was so focused on everything he did, and it had to be done perfectly. Sometimes he'd catch me watching him and make some silly remark— *"Like what you see?"* — and flirt.

Flirting was normal for him and me. It was too easy for us because we knew that we were solid. I was attracted to him; he was so handsome. His soul was even more beautiful.

Some of the kids at school assumed we were together. I didn't try to date anyone, and neither did Myles. One time, Piper Evans asked him out, and he just laughed in her face. "No way" was his response.

I watched the entire thing, and the petty part of me was so glad at his reaction. I still hated her.

Later, he told me that even though she was kind of cute, there was no way he'd ever date her because of what she did back in fifth grade. At this point, even I was over what Piper had said to me that day, but I wasn't going to try to persuade Myles to think any differently. I'm pretty sure he was trying to make me jealous with his "she's kind of cute" comment.

"Thank you for bringing my Ford back to life, Mr. Ford," I said when we heard the rumble of the engine.

"Should we, uh, test it out?" he asked, praying, I'm sure, that I would agree.

"Grandpa just left for the bar. Should be hours before he's back."

"Let's do it."

We high-five, and I hop into my Bronco. The interior isn't in bad condition. It just smells like dust and, oddly, faintly of my mother. I sit there for a minute, remembering the last time I was in this car. I hadn't known what was going on or that my beautiful life was about to turn into something so painful.

"I know where we should go," I tell Myles. I was able to restart my art collection and have already sold two of my art pieces to a couple of shops around town. It's not much, but I have enough money for some gas and a ferry ride.

He puts on his sunglasses and nods. "Let's hit it, girl." He smiles and sticks his arm out the window.

I drive to the ferry and pay the fee.

Myles and I watch the ocean over the rail, just as my mother and I did so many years ago. We don't see any sea life, just the ripples the giant boat leaves behind.

After disembarking, we pull up to a small light-blue house. The grass is incredibly tall, weeds have taken over, and the vines on the sides of the house are overgrown and dead-looking. There's a FOR SALE sign that's barely hanging on in front of the house.

"Jeez," I say as we get out of the Bronco.

Myles follows me. "Is this where you used to live?" he asks, assuming that is why we are here.

"Yeah, it is. I wonder why no one has bought it."

I close my eyes for a moment and remember a better time.

It was Christmas, and we had cut down a small tree from down the road. Mom and I decorated it with pinecones, dried flowers, and sprigs of colorful weeds. It didn't need extravagant, store-bought ornaments to be beautiful. There were a few presents under the tree, all for me.

Mom had the biggest smile on her face and was making waffles for us. I remember falling asleep with a full belly after gift opening.

We open the door to see all the furniture still where it was left. Obviously covered in dust and dirt, and I see a plethora of spiderwebs in every corner.

"I mean, I see potential, but I also see why no one is super interested in buying it," Myles says. "It hasn't been taken care of."

His comment hits me a little bit hard. *Kind of like me,* I think. "I loved this place so much; maybe it's cursed now," I respond pessimistically.

We walk all around the house and stop in my old bedroom. Even though it's a dusty mess, the mural has stayed vibrant. We make our way to the backyard. Everything is overgrown, and somehow the flowers have died, even in their desired weather. Maybe the weeds infiltrated them and suffocated them all to death.

A sudden burst of emotion hits me, and I drop to my knees on the ground. "Maybe she's dead," I say in between cries.

"Penny, we don't know that; we don't know what happened," Myles says, kneeling with me and holding me in his arms. "I sincerely hope we find out what did happen though. I know you need that. I know you need closure and an answer to all the whys," he continues as he strokes my hair.

We. He said "we" as if we are a team, as if he isn't someone who is going to leave me or hurt me.

I look up at him, our faces incredibly close; most of my tears have disappeared. "Thank you. Thank you for everything."

"I don't know if you have noticed, but I would do anything for you, Miss Penelope Wolfe," he says smiling.

My stomach flutters, and I can't think of a better time than now to kiss him.

So I do.

Chapter Four

Senior year was mediocre; two of the four classes I took were electives. Luckily, one of them was art. Although boredom was a common feeling during my last year of high school, I was grateful to be taking a class I loved. Plus, being out of the house was a perk.

My first kiss was exactly what I imagined it to be, with exactly whom I imagined it to be. We didn't talk about it after it happened, not even once. I think we both wanted to hold that memory in a protected capsule. It was as if, were we to speak of it, the capsule would open, and some of its elements would be tainted.

I know deep down we both want something more. I know we crave it, but the fear of jeopardizing our friendship for a label is greater.

We graduated last week. Julianne and Lacey planned a lunch today on Main Street; we wanted to get together one last time before we all went on to whatever we had planned next.

"I'll be moving at the end of summer," Julianne announced. "I was accepted into Columbia!" She squealed.

I was happy for her; she was the smartest person I knew and deserved to be in a huge city full of opportunities.

"What about you, Penny?" she asked me.

"I really want to focus on my art, maybe travel a little bit," I told her.

"Well, you're the best artist I know, so I think that's a great idea," Lacey chimed in. "I'm going to hang out at home for a while, work for the summer, get a job, and see where it leads me," she said, taking a bite of her sandwich.

We finished our food and said our goodbyes. We promised each other we would try to hang out one more time before Julianne left for college.

I was just about to get into my Bronco and head home when I heard his voice.

"Hey, you"—Myles slid up behind me and twirled me around so we were face-to-face—"I got you something." He held out his hand.

A little red box.

"For what?" I asked him, taking the box from his palm.

"For your birthday, an early gift."

I give him a smile and open the box. Inside is a silver chain with a light-purple flower pendant. It's beautiful. The silver gleams in the sun when I move it around, and the pendant is a dainty anemone flower. One of my favorites.

I look at Myles. He's sporting such a genuine smile, staring at me excitedly and waiting for my response.

"I love it!" I jump and give him the biggest thank-you hug. I unclasp the necklace and motion for him to put it on for me as I turn around.

He reaches over me. The pendant sits flush with my skin. He clasps it together and moves my hair back into place. "I noticed you didn't have any jewelry, and apparently every girl needs some sparkle. I thought who, other than her best friend, should give her some?" He adds, "Also, I have plans for us tonight. I'll pick you up."

"Okay, but we have to wait until he's asleep," I respond, referring to my grandfather.

"I know." Myles nods. "I have a few errands to run; text me as soon as he's out." He winks at me and makes his way to his truck, a few parking spots over.

Grandpa is still a nightmare, but he has slowed down a bit. I'm quicker than he now and smarter. I have gotten better at lying, which deters his potential outbursts.

It's been about six months since the last time he hit me. I never told Myles about that; he thinks the physical abuse stopped much longer ago. I feel bad keeping that information from him, but Myles doesn't have any more patience for what Grandpa does to me. He told me that, the next time it happened, he was going to give Grandpa what he deserves. I fear the result of that, so I keep it from him.

As I get ready for whatever Myles has planned for us, I have the urge to look nice, so I pick out my favorite yellow sundress. It will look perfect with my new necklace. I was never really trained in how to do my hair in anything other than a bun or ponytail, so I leave it down and put on some mascara. I add a little blush and a tad of lipstick. Not that I am trying to impress Myles; but, then again, I kind of am.

Grandpa got me a prepaid phone a few months ago; he said I needed it to apply to colleges and find out where I am going next. He has no idea that I have no plans for college, but I accepted the phone anyways.

I have much bigger plans, like selling enough art pieces to rent my own space where I can teach painting and ceramics classes. I just need enough to get on my feet; then I think I could really take off.

I peek my head outside of my room and hear Grandpa snoring in his bedroom. *Good to go.*

Penny: He's out!

Myles: Meet me out front.

I quietly step down the stairs and go out the back door, which is much quieter than the front door. I see Myles sitting in his truck, grinning at me. My best friend has the best smile.

"Hi, you," I greet him, returning his same flirtatious remark from earlier.

"And hi to you," he says flirtatiously, eyeing me up and down.

"Oh stop." I nudge him.

"Ready?"

"You bet."

Anything that I get to do with Myles is exactly what I want to be doing. We don't have to even be doing anything. It may be unhealthy that most of my happiness lives with him, but I'm okay with it. *What do I have to lose?*

He drives us about twenty minutes out of town and into a little nook in the forest. Port Townsend is part of the Pacific Northwest and is surrounded by the Olympic National Forest. There is beautiful scenery everywhere you go. This specific nook ends right before a cliff overlooking the ocean, but it's still surrounded by dense green trees.

Myles backs in so we can sit in the bed of the truck. He lays two big plush blankets in the back and sets a basket on top of them. "I know; it's cheesy," he says as he opens the basket to show me three different kinds of cheese and a variety of crackers. He gets his humor from his father.

I laugh as we get into the bed of the truck and settle in. *How cute is this?*

"What are you doing, Myles? This feels like a date," I say while digging into the basket.

"It's not; it's just two friends hanging out. Although, I do have to admit, you look beautiful, Penelope," he says to me, handing me a can of Pepsi.

I blush and feel my body warm up.

Myles has complimented me before. Sometimes, they are genuine compliments; other times, it's flirtatious banter. But tonight it feels a little different.

I like when he calls me Penelope. Mostly everyone calls me Penny, which I don't hate...but it feels special when he says my full name.

"Thank you," I shyly respond, trying to make sense of the current mood.

We enjoy each other's presence, along with some cheese and crackers and the faint sound of the ocean waves. If I could sit in this spot forever, I'd never complain.

The noises of nature are interrupted by Myles. " I signed up for the fire academy a few weeks ago," he tells me in the middle of biting into a cracker.

"What?! Myles! That's amazing!" I say excitedly.

"Yeah, I guess so," he says sadly.

"Aren't you happy about it?"

"Well, yeah. Not everyone gets accepted; that's why I didn't say anything when I applied."

"So when do you find out if you are in?"

"I found out this morning. I'm in." He pauses, and before I can congratulate him, he delivers the reason why he is not excited. "I have to move to Seattle."

I feel a stab in my heart. I think of the day we sat in the backyard of my Coupeville home; I told myself then that he wasn't someone who was going to leave me as everyone else has. Yet, here we sit, exactly that happening.

I don't remember a life without Myles. We've been each other's whole world for seven years. We haven't spent more than one week apart, and that was only when he was off on family trips.

I didn't realize that this day would be here so soon. "When do you leave?" I ask him, no longer able to eat.

He takes a deep breath and exhales slowly. "Tomorrow," he forces himself to say.

Tomorrow?!

"The other guy they selected backed out at the last second, and I was next in line. That's why I gave you an early birthday present and wanted to spend the night with you." His expression is that of a sad puppy. "I feel like I shouldn't even be going. It feels wrong." He hangs his head low.

I think of my words before I speak; I can't say the wrong thing during such a fragile moment. I want to scream at him and ask how he could leave me like this, but I feel that would be wrong to do. We can't be neighbors forever, and this is his opportunity to make something of himself. I am his friend before anything, and that means I unconditionally support him in all ways, and will forever.

I reach out and place my hand on his. "It's not wrong, Myles. You have earned this; it's your time to go and become the person you want to be. You should be proud of yourself; I know I am proud of you," I reassure him, trying to hide the pain and unwanted anger I am feeling.

"Seattle isn't far. We can visit each other and call each other; hell, we could even write letters to each other," I tell him, my hand still on his.

He nods in agreement.

Seattle is only a couple of hours away, and the fire academy doesn't last forever. We will just have to be patient and pray that the time and distance don't force us to drift apart.

"Penny?" he says, placing his other hand over mine.

I look up at him, and his eyes are almost in tears. I squeeze both of his hands.

"Penny...I love you," he says, almost whispering.

I freeze.

The last person who told me they loved me was my mother. Nearly ten years ago.

"I've loved you since the day I saw you whack Piper Evans in the face." He chuckles, trying to make light of what he just told me.

I don't need to say those words back to him right now; instead...I show him. I lean in and kiss him. I taste the hint of soda on his breath and feel his hands slide up my arms, then to my face, holding it gently. Our delicate kisses turn into passionate ones. His tongue is strong and warm, and his movements match mine.

I pull my dress up over my head, and he follows with his shirt and then his jeans. We continue to undress between kisses, until we are eventually completely naked and lying down. He moves to hover over me, breathing heavily. He's never looked more beautiful than right now in this moment. His sandy-blond hair covers part of his blue eyes and his cheeks, which are rosy red.

He slowly comes closer and gives me another kiss, this time sliding himself into me. The gentle, synchronized moves of our bodies are everything. We are angels swimming in a serene bed of clouds, and this is my heaven.

Chapter Five

Making love to Myles was everything it was supposed to be. It was what girls dream of for their first time. He was patient, being that this was the first time for both of us. It was slow and gentle, yet still so full of love and passion.

After, we lie next to each other for a while. Seeing the starlit skies through the tops of the trees makes it even better. We lie together in silence, my head nestled into the crevice of his neck.

This is the best night of my life thus far.

The day after was the absolute worst.

I woke up early to catch Myles before he left. He had his truck packed, was ready to go by 6:00 a.m., and was waiting for me to say one last goodbye. I snuck out of the house and ran into his arms. We held each other so tightly in a hug, both crying.

My world was crashing down, and I felt as if I should jump into the ocean and never come up for air. I was suffocating, drowning, and dying from the inside out, all rolled into one feeling. I could feel that Myles was too.

It was less than fair that he was leaving. Not because he chose to leave. The universe was just so cruel as to give him to me, only to take him away again.

We released each other from our hug. I looked up at him and, in words, admitted, "I love you too," before watching him get into his truck.

I stood in the middle of the road, watching him drive away. Every inch farther he went, an extra mile of pain filled my bones.

At one point, I saw his brake lights turn on, as if he had forgotten something or maybe had changed his mind. But, almost immediately, he continued on his way.

I wanted to trust that he would come back for me, but it's so easy for people to drift apart when they are living two different lives.

"Goodbye," I whispered to myself.

I stood in that road for what felt like hours. I was dreading the fact that I had to walk back into my house and go on with my day as if my world hadn't just been torn apart. Not to mention, every day after that until he returned. *If he returned.*

I wished my mother were here to hold me through this heartbreak; even Grandma would have been better than nothing. I tried to focus my mind on what that would feel like.

I run into her arms, and let her hold me while I cry into her body. She runs her fingers through my hair and tells me that it will all be okay.

I almost instantly returned from that mind movie. I cried as I walked up the steps and into the dreadful place I called home. I opened the front door, and Grandpa was standing there.

"What the hell was that!" he yelled.

My guess is that he is still drunk from last night. "Myles left today. I was saying goodbye," I told him, still sobbing.

"Have you been fucking that kid?! I'll be damned if I have some teen mom under my roof, with a fucking bastard baby," he screamed.

"What is wrong with you! Why do you hate me so much?!" I screamed back. Nothing he could say or do would hurt more than Myles's leaving.

He tried though. He grabbed me by the hair and slammed my head against the door panel. Before I could steady myself, he held my shoulder up with one hand and then proceeded to punch me in the stomach multiple times.

"That ought a kill whatever's in there," he said. Leaving me huddled against the wall, he walked out the front door, got in his truck, and drove away.

That is the last time he is ever going to touch me. I'm turning eighteen in two months; I don't have to be here anymore. Myles is gone. I have no reason to stay.

I packed everything I could. Clothes, my art supplies, my artwork. I grabbed a toothbrush, a hairbrush, pillows, and blankets. I went to Grandpa's room and ransacked every drawer and corner until I found some money stashed in his sock drawer. I made sure to throw everything across the room, including my phone, so he knew I had been there.

So no one can find me.

I shoved everything into the back of my Bronco. I hopped in and turned it on, breathing heavily. Fear, loss, the uncertainty of what was next caught up with me in the moment.

I slammed my hands on the steering wheel and screamed at the top of my lungs. I caught a glimpse of my forehead in the rearview mirror—blood trickled down my temple.

It doesn't look too bad. I'll be okay.

I heard the closing of a screen door and saw Vicky standing on the porch in a robe. "Penelope are you okay?" she yelled towards me.

I wished I could run to her; I knew she would hold me the way I so badly needed. She'd probably let me stay with her and figure out a way to take me away from Grandpa until I was an adult. Instead, I just looked at her.

Her eyes widened when she saw the blood on my face.

I forced myself to give her a sad smile; then I put the Bronco in Reverse and drove away. My body ached with pain. Physically because of the beating I was just given, and emotionally because of the heartache. But for the first time in forever, I felt free.

I had nothing left to lose.

I wasn't sure where I was going. All I knew was that the farther away I went, the safer I felt. No one could ever leave me again if I left now. I wouldn't dare let anyone get too close to me from here on out. I was going as far as the money I found would take me.

CHAPTER SIX

SIX MONTHS LATER

I wake up to a heavy tapping on my back window. I open my eyes to find a police officer peeking through the dirty glass.

"Ma'am, you can't sleep here," she says, shaking her head.

I rush to get up and slide myself into the driver's seat. I open the car door and get out. "I'm so sorry. I was just so tired from driving last night that I thought it would best to pull over," I lie and then attempt to straighten out my messy hair.

She scans me from the bottom of my bare feet to the top of my tangled head. "How old are you?"

"I'm eighteen," I respond truthfully this time.

She sighs. "Well, you can't sleep here. I'm sure your mother is worried about you. Go on home," she says and walks back to her patrol car.

My mother is most definitely not worried about me.

I take a moment to admire my view. The deep-indigo ocean stretches out as far as I can see, the sky is blue, and the sun is awake. I inhale and let the salty air fill my lungs. I take a few steps forward and feel that the endless aisle of sand is still warm from yesterday's heat.

I've been dodging cops for the last six months. I try to move my car around a lot, so they don't see it parked in the same spot, but it's getting harder as time goes on. I've been to pretty much every beach parking lot within a fifteen-mile radius, and my car stands out.

You'd think an old Bronco would blend into a beach town, but I guess that is reserved for old VW Buses and Priuses.

I applied for an apartment in Pacific Beach last week and should hear today whether I have been approved or not. It belongs to a nice elderly couple I met at work. They mentioned that they had an apartment they were renting out. They told me I reminded them of their granddaughter up in Los Angeles, and that as long as I pass the background check, they would love to rent it to me.

I didn't mention to them that I was homeless, living in a car that used to belong to my missing mother. Or that I fled Washington state in order to get out of an abusive home. Not that it's any of their business, but, stereotypically, I'd be considered a hoodlum and probably wouldn't be rented to.

I've been working at a restaurant called Coral's Café. It's an American-style restaurant that sits right on Garnet Avenue. It can get super busy, so the tips are really good.

I walked in there a couple of days after arriving in San Diego and asked if they were hiring. They had been short-staffed and pretty much hired me on the spot. So I've been saving up every dollar I earn in order to be able to stop living in my car.

I watched as the police officer drove off. Then I checked my phone—9:30 a.m. I need to be at work in an hour.

I got a new phone shortly after I ended up here. It was one of the only things I spent the money I stole on, besides gas and food. No one back home has my phone number, and if I were being honest with myself, I'd say that is a good thing. I want to be a ghost.

There is only one person whom I would like to confide in and vent to, but he is on his way to a better life. Who am I to even think of interrupting that? I hate myself every day for not finding Myles and explaining to him why I disappeared.

I hope his mom didn't call him and tell him what she saw that morning. I don't think she would have done that. She knew, if he found out, he would turn around, race back, and risk losing the opportunity to fulfill his dream in order to help an almost-nobody girl.

Cutting ties seemed to be the best choice for everyone at the time. So far, that has proven to be true.

I grabbed my shower bag out of the back seat of the Bronco. I've learned to be pretty organized due to my lack of space. I found a compartmental bag at Walmart; it holds all my toiletries and folds up super small, so I can tuck it under the passenger seat. My clothes are folded neatly in a duffel bag that I keep in the back, and I've managed to establish a comfortable sleeping situation.

Most of the beach parking lots have bathrooms with showers you can use for a few quarters. So that's what I do. I don't mind them either; most people leave me alone, and the water is never cold. But, then again, the weather is always perfect here, so nothing ever really feels cold.

I brush my wet hair and pull it up into a clip. I put on some makeup, jean shorts, and a white T-shirt. Coral's Café has a very relaxed ambiance, so shorts and a tee are perfect work attire.

The restaurant was already getting crowded when I walked in. The manager, Mike, gives me a *"thank God you're here"* look when I came in the back door.

"Hey, hon." Amelia greets me with a kiss on the cheek as she rushes by me, carrying a plate of French toast. Amelia Jones is my coworker and my only friend out here. She's a freckly brunette with a whole lot of energy.

I put my backpack in my cubby in the back room and quickly tie a black apron around my waist. I immediately dive into the brunch rush; one of the waitresses called in sick, so nearly half of the tables have been waiting for service much longer than desired. Which means there are quite a few hungry and upset people here.

I'm pretty good at calming angry patrons down. I think it stems from tiptoeing around Grandpa while growing up, trying to manipulate my words into something that would ease the tension. Plus, I typically throw in a free meal.

Brunch is my favorite, probably because it's my first meal of the day. Since I've been trying to save most of my money, I usually wait to eat until I get to work; I eat for free.

"So…any word on the new place?" Amelia asks me. She sits on the barstool next to me, chugging a glass of water during our quick break.

"No, not yet." I shake my head.

"It'll happen. I don't know anyone more deserving than you." She smiles at me. Amelia knows the general story of my childhood. She knows that my mom left, that my best friend was a guy, and that I live in my car.

She doesn't know about Grandpa. I fear that would come off as a weakness, or that I would be seen as a fragile little girl.

My phone buzzes. Speak of the devil—a 619 area code—someone local is calling.

I look over at Amelia. "Can you cover me for five minutes? It's the Bostics!"

She gives me a thumbs-up. I swear she's a good-luck charm. Every time she reassures me that something will work out, it does.

"Hello?" I say as I answer the phone.

"Penelope. Hi, sweetie, it's Trudy Bostic." The older woman on the other end of the phone continues, "Everything came back clear, so we are more than happy to write up an agreement for you."

I quietly jump up and down with excitement. "Oh, I'm so happy. Thank you, Mrs. Bostic."

"Oh please, call me Trudy. Could you come by this evening to sign everything?"

"Absolutely. I'll come by right after work. Thank you again, Trudy."

"Bye-bye now," she says and hangs up.

FINALLY! These last six months have been pretty rough. As much as I love my Bronco, it's not meant for sleeping in on a nightly basis.

Amelia pops her head in. "How'd it go?"

"I got it!" I squeal, and we both jump up and down with happiness.

She gives me a tight hug. "I told you it would work out," she says, smiling.

After my shift, I hurry over to the Bostics' house. I've been there once before when I dropped off my application. They live in a big house in La Jolla, which is only about fifteen minutes from Pacific Beach. Mr. Bostic used to be a band manager, so it's safe to say his retirement treats him well.

They kept the lease signing short and sweet. Some signed documents and a handover of keys, and I'm on my way to my new apartment. I promised to treat the place as if it were my own, and that's exactly what I plan to do.

What a foreign feeling—a place all to my own. A safe and comfortable dwelling. A *home*.

The apartment is in a smaller building. I think there are only ten units, but it has its own laundry room and a nice community pool. As I open the door to my new home, I take in the fresh-paint smell.

Wow.

The walls are beige with white trim, and the floors are a blond wood. It's nothing like my house back in Coupeville; it's less earthy, more modern, and it's definitely not like Grandpa's house, which is all I could have asked for. It's just right for me.

My mind wanders back to Myles. Before this very moment, the only times I've ever felt completely safe were with Mom and him. I went to the local library a few times and tried searching for him on social media. I wanted to see how he was doing. Did he graduate from the academy? Did he get a girlfriend? I wasn't able to find him online, so I just tell myself that he is happy somewhere. I hope that's the truth.

For a while I was almost sick to my stomach, missing him and wondering what he thought of my disappearance. I felt so terrible that there was no closure. Our goodbye was temporary when we said it; neither of us knew that would turn out to be the last time we ever saw each other.

Although, if we had known, I'm not sure it would have changed much. Our last night together was perfect.

My thoughts are interrupted by a voice behind me. "Hi there, we just wanted to stop by and introduce ourselves."

I turn, and there is a couple standing in the open doorway of the apartment next to mine. "Oh hi, I'm Penny." I walk to them and shake their hands.

"I'm Sandra, and this is Jose," Sandra says, pointing to the man standing next to her.

"It's nice to meet you both," I say, smiling.

"We live right next door, so if you ever need anything, let us know," Jose says.

"Thank you, I appreciate that."

Sandra gives me a piece of paper with her and Jose's number on it. After they leave, I put it under a magnet on the fridge.

The Bostics offered the apartment almost completely furnished. In the bedroom, there is a full-sized bed with a dresser and a small walk-in closet. The combination living/dining room has a couch, a coffee table, a round dining table, and four chairs. I have enough money saved up to buy a TV and maybe a bookcase. I can't wait to decorate and add my own personal touches to make it feel more like my own place.

Unpacking didn't take very long. I was able to wash all of my clothes and put them away. I used most of the closet space to store my art supplies and a few small pieces that I had finished during the last few months.

I plop on my sheetless bed and stare at the ceiling.

I deserve this.

Pacific Beach is an active section of San Diego. Locals and tourists both fill the streets at all times of the year. I hear chatter and laughter outside my bedroom window, which doesn't bother me one bit; it's oddly comforting. In fact, I watch the passersby and try to eavesdrop on their conversations. So far, it's mostly younger people walking by, talking about their weekend plans or the new vegan spot they found downtown.

There is a lot to do out here, and there are a lot of artsy and creative people. Now that I have the space to paint, I'm going to make a website and try to get my work out there. I'll go visit the library on my next day off and see what I can do.

I do miss being in Washington; nothing here can beat the beauty up there. The beaches and sunsets are charming, and the salty air that gifts you the perfect breeze is great and all, but it's almost too cliché for me.

I love the hidden wonders in the forests, like finding a beautiful yellow fungus growing under a fallen tree and watching the banana slugs make it a shelter from the random bursts of rain.

Sounds like a good art piece idea. The thoughts of vibrant rainforests make my stomach pang.

A comforting ache. I'm grateful that I have the ability to keep those memories alive in my art.

Chapter Seven

"How about this?" Amelia asks, holding up a miniature crystal-cat figurine.

"Um…" I respond, trying to think of a way to let her down easy.

"I'm just kidding," she says, rolling her eyes and putting it back down.

We have been driving around Pacific Beach all day, finding yard sales and thrift shops. I've got my apartment fixed up almost to my satisfaction; it's just missing a few cute trinkets for the final touches.

I find a piece of wall art that I am going to put out on my patio. It's a bronze sun; it's already weathered and will look nice above my beige egg chair.

"Oh yeah, that's *so* you," Amelia says, admiring my choice.

I nod in agreement and find the homeowner to make my purchase.

"My mom just called; she wants to have us over for lunch," Amelia says as we are leaving the yard sale.

"Us?" I ask to clarify.

"Of course. You're like my best friend now. Besides, she makes the best BLTs."

"I could go for one of those."

She grins and gestures for me to hop in the front seat of her bright-red Toyota Camry.

Amelia is a few years older than I am; she has lived in San Diego her whole life. She's talked about her family a few times. I know that she has both her mom and dad and a little brother who's eight years old.

Her parents live in a small house on the outskirts of town. The lawn is maintained, but cluttered with various ocean-life statues and a pair of colorful surfboards that are rested against the side of the house. It reminds me of a scene from a surfer movie; the other houses on the street follow suit.

A little boy comes running out of the front door and leaps into Amelia's arms. "Mia!" he shouts.

She greets him with a tight squeeze and sets him back on the ground. She rustles his hair. "Have you grown since the last time I saw you?" she jokes.

"I saw you, like, two weeks ago," he says sarcastically.

"Kaiden, this is my friend Penny," Amelia introduces us.

"Hi, Kaiden, is that your surfboard over there?" I ask, pointing to the boards.

"Yeah. Me and my dad surf a lot. Are you scared of sharks?" he asks enthusiastically.

"Yes, I am afraid of sharks," I admit.

"You shouldn't be; they are so cool. I found a shark's tooth last weekend. Do you want to see it?" His expression is begging for me to say yes.

"Absolutely," I say and follow him into the house.

An older woman is in the kitchen, cooking bacon. "Hey, Mom," Amelia says, shutting the screen door.

"Hey, girls." She smiles and comes over to give us both a hug. "You must be Penny. My name is Leslie," she says, releasing her hug.

"It's nice to meet you. Thanks for inviting me."

"Anytime. Make yourself at home, sweetie." She heads back into the kitchen to finish prepping lunch.

Kaiden has been tugging on my arm this whole time for me to go see his shark's tooth. Amelia whispers, "Have fun," and plops on the couch.

I follow him into his room and admire the various pictures and beach-shell chaos scattered throughout the room. He opens a drawer in his dresser and pulls out a box. "See?" he says after he opens it.

It's a perfectly white and frighteningly large shark's tooth. "Wow, that's the real deal," I say, taking it out of the box to study it. "What kind of shark do you think it's from?"

"Probably a great white; it's pretty big," he says and puts it back in the box. He stands next to me while I continue to admire his collections. "Do you have a brother?"

"No, I don't have any siblings." *Not that I know of, at least.*

"That must have been a boring childhood," he blurts.

Boring? I wish.

Leslie calls from the kitchen, letting us know that lunch is ready. When we join the others, Kaiden and I find everyone sitting at the table, including Amelia's father. He's handsome in a scruffy-surfer way.

He smiles. "Hi, I'm Finn." He shakes my hand from across the table.

"Hi." I return his smile and take my seat.

Amelia wasn't lying when she said her mom makes the best BLTs. She made the bread from scratch and got the lettuce and tomatoes from a local farmer. "Always support local," she commented during lunch.

Kaiden and Finn told us about the surf session they had that morning and about all the dolphins they saw. Kaiden was adorable and showed excitement about everything.

I envied being able to cherish life like that. I was happy for this kid. He had a family who loved him and enjoyed spending time with him. He didn't feel that he was burden; he knew that he was an important part of the family.

Leslie told me the story of how she and Finn met. They were both surfing down in Mexico, and Finn hit a pretty rough wave and banged his head on a rock. Leslie saw it happen, dragged him out of the water, and gave him CPR. About a year later, Amelia was born.

When Leslie got pregnant, she stopped surfing and hasn't gotten back on a board since. "I guess I passed that talent on to Kaiden," she said, smiling sweetly at her young boy.

Finn looked so lovingly at his wife when she told their love story. "She saved my life. If I hadn't had a concussion, I would have asked her to marry me right then and there," he chimed in.

After lunch, I was given a tour of Finn's garage. He collects all kinds of things he finds on the beach, including a whole tub full of engagement rings and abandoned jewelry.

"That was my best investment." He points to a metal detector in the corner. "I find so much stuff out there. I hold on to it for a while, in case I hear of anyone looking for lost jewelry, but once some time passes, I go ahead and sell it." He rests his hands on his hips. "It funds all of our family vacations."

Family vacation—what a lovely concept that is.

"That's pretty cool," I say, admiring the tub full of sparkles.

"Kaiden finds the cooler stuff. I'm sure he showed you his shark's tooth."

"Oh yes. I saw that first thing."

We chuckle together.

Leslie joins us in the garage. "Penny, thank you for coming over today. We have just loved having you here." She smiles. "Amelia told me you don't have family in town. I just wanted to let you know that you are welcome anytime, including all holidays." She embraces me.

I take a second to enjoy the coconut aroma of her hair. I can see why Finn is so in love with her. She's beautiful, caring and incredibly motherly.

"I really appreciate that. Thank you, Leslie," I say, trying to hold back a happy tear.

Amelia pops her head in. "Ready to head out?"

I nod and join her outside. I thank Leslie and Finn again for their hospitality and give a high five to Kaiden.

"Will you come back?" he asks me as I get into the car.

I smile at him. "I would love to come back."

We wave goodbye as we drive off.

"You have a great family."

"I love them to pieces, and they seem to really like you. I think I may have finally found my sister from another mister." She giggles, pulls her sunglasses over her eyes, and turns up the music.

I wish I could tell her just how happy that makes me; having a sister—having any sort of family, in fact—is a dream to me. Who knows? I may have one out there somewhere, but having Amelia is even better. She *chose* me.

I roll down the window and close my eyes, enjoying the warm air touching my skin. I imagine summer barbecues and family beach days full of delicious food and wholesomeness. I remember, not that long ago, imagining opportunities like that with Myles and his family.

Maybe I've been given another chance...maybe I don't have to be alone.

Chapter Eight

Three Years Later

Today is my twenty-first birthday, and, naturally, I am pessimistic. I don't love it when attention is on me; it makes me feel as if I have to put on a façade to please other people. Up until I met Amelia, my birthdays were always low-key.

I spent most of my morning painting and enjoying the nice summer breeze that comes in through the door to my balcony.

A short time ago, I took the awkward leap and created a website and a social media page dedicated to my artwork. It feels odd to build myself up online, maybe because I often feel that my work is not good enough, and I fear the negative feedback that I could receive. Everyone is braver behind a screen, including me apparently.

Fortunately, I've had a lot of traffic on both pages and have even sold a few pieces to people who were willing to pay for packing and shipping.

I've also been frequenting a few local art events and have sold some pieces in those as well. Not nearly enough to quit my job at Coral's Café anytime soon, but it's nice to know that people admire my work and want to take a piece of it home with them.

It's almost toxic how focused I have been these last couple of years. I work, I paint, I work, and then I paint some more. Sometimes I'll go to the art studio downtown and use their kiln, trying to keep my pottery skills sharp. Most of the coffee mugs I own are the ones that I have made, and whenever Amelia comes over, she tries to steal one. I'm glad she appreciates them.

Amelia forces me out of the apartment on a weekly basis; in her mind, work shouldn't consume me. So I do have somewhat of a social life. She's big on spending a lot of time at the beach, which makes sense, being that she was born into a surfing family. Most of the time, we are out by the ocean, or at her parents' house, helping her dad list jewelry online and eating some of Leslie's delicious home-cooked meals. They have pretty much adopted me at this point. I've spent every Thanksgiving, Christmas, and other major holiday with them since we met.

Leslie is the kind of mom who knows the balance between parenting and friendship. She can nurture and give solid life advice, and at the same time, you can talk to her as if she were one of the girls. Being that we are all adults, she's pretty involved in Amelia's scandalous adventures.

Amelia's a player and has a new boyfriend every other week. I always feel a little bummed when she's on to the next one. I feel bad for the guys. Amelia's easy to love, and they realize that quickly, but she's already over them before they even know what hit them. She tells me that life is too short to settle. If she finds one flaw in a guy, she's out. It's not hard to believe, considering her example of love. Leslie and Finn's love story is a tough one to beat, and it's not wrong to search for *the* one.

I envy Amelia's boldness, confidence, and absolute trust that she will make sound decisions. I tend to second-guess myself when coming to a bump in the road; I weigh every scenario and play movies in my head. I'm always waiting for the rug to be pulled out from under me, which makes any type of confidence almost impossible. My love life is nearly nonexistent.

The only action that I've gotten was my neighbor Jose's brother, Marco, asking me out a few months back. I was hesitant to go out with my neighbor's brother. But he was cute, and I was feeling a little desperate, so I went.

He asked me to meet him at this bougie steakhouse in La Jolla. I even bought a new dress for the occasion. It was a pale-pink dress that went down to my knees; it hugged every curve perfectly. I was actually really excited to dress up and go out, but before I even sat at the table, his girlfriend came running through the restaurant, yelling and screaming at him. I left immediately and didn't turn back, even though I kind of wanted to witness the drama.

I also returned the dress.

I don't think Marco is allowed to go over to his brother's place anymore. Thankfully, I haven't bumped into him. I'd rather keep awkward situations to a minimum.

After that experience, I tossed the idea of finding a guy. Besides being physically deprived, I don't really need a man. I'm doing okay by myself, and my focus is on making my art into a career; that takes self-discipline and time, both of which a boyfriend would take away from.

Against my wishes, Amelia and some of the girls at work decided to throw me a little birthday dinner at work, tonight after closing. They told me it would be low-key and casual, so I put on my favorite jeans shorts and flowy white top. I plucked a flower from the planters by the parking lot and tucked it behind my ear before heading out.

The girls decorated one of the tables with balloons and colorful streamers; island music was blaring throughout the building. The chef made my favorite—macaroni and cheese—but with an extra ingredient.

"Lobster?" I ask, looking at the bits of crustacean in my bowl.

"Try it; it's amazing," Sid, the main chef, says to me.

You'd think, after living near the ocean most of my life and working at this café, I would have tried lobster by now, but this is the first time for me.

I take a bite, and to my surprise, it is delicious. "Oh yum, this is fantastic," I say to him, taking an even bigger bite.

"Told you." He winks and serves up some more dishes for everyone else.

"We also got you a gift," Amelia says, handing me a purple gift bag full of white tissue paper.

"This is really sweet, guys; you didn't have to do this," I say, opening it.

I uncover a clear-resin palette with real pressed flowers embedded in it. It is gorgeous. "This is so beautiful!" I say excitedly.

I get up and hug and thank each one of them. I hate to admit it, but this is exactly what I needed on my birthday. The kindness of dedicating a night to me and the well-thought-out gift made my glum perspective much brighter. I would have been okay with staying at home and going to bed as early as I could to try to get the day over with, but Amelia begged and insisted that I get out tonight. I'm glad she did.

Amelia also invited some of her other friends. I'd met a few of them here and there when we went out, but she and her family are pretty much the only people I spend my time with outside of work. I've kept my promise to myself to not allow people to grow too close to me. Even Amelia doesn't know the true depths and aches of my soul.

As the night progressed, so did the number of people. Our little birthday dinner turned into a full-fledged party. My anxiety trickled in, but I decided to grab a drink, rather than ditch my own party.

Some of the guys moved a few tables around and created a makeshift dance floor, which turned out to be very popular. After my second drink, even I—introverted Penny—was out there, shimmying about.

I wondered if this is what college parties looked like. I was okay with my decision to skip that adventure in my life. I could have figured out student loans and payment plans if I had wanted to, but my goal is something money can't buy. I don't want to be confined by the laws of a mundane working society. I want the freedom that comes with being an artist—no rules governing my work and my creations freely interpreted subjectively and differently by every observer.

Out of breath, I leave the dance floor and find an empty table. Soon, Amelia is walking towards me with a man who has black, slicked-back hair. I don't recognize him, but immediately notice how good-looking he is.

"Pen, meet Ben," she says, giggling at her rhyme.

"Hi, Pen," he says, holding his hand out for a handshake.

"It's Penny," I say, returning his handshake while rolling my eyes at Amelia.

"I like Penny better," he says, smiling.

"Oh my God. Penny and Benny." Amelia bursts out laughing.

Okay, she's totally drunk.

I like to enjoy a drink here and there, but I know my limits and stop when I need to, so drink number three is the end for me. The first time I went to a house party with Amelia, I learned my limit very quickly. I was so drunk I passed out on the patio. When I woke up, I was disgusted with myself. I felt like Grandpa—a drunk and a mess. It was a terrible feeling. So, now, two to three drinks are my max.

Amelia clumsily bumps into a table. "Oh man, I gotta pee," she says, leaving Ben and me alone.

I suck at small talk, so I take a sip of my drink and watch the guys at the other end of the restaurant arm wrestle.

"I hear it's your birthday," Ben says, breaking the silence.

"Yes, it is," I respond nervously.

"You look a little too young to be drinking."

"Does that bother you?"

"I'm just curious if you're old enough to be drinking."

Why does he care?

I turn to him for the first time since being left alone. I'm instantly drawn to his dark eyes. "Are you a cop?" I ask with a little bit sarcasm.

"No, I'm a lawyer." He grins.

He looks at me and smiles. He has a dimple on his cheek, but only on the left side. I watch him as he obviously goes from looking at my face, to looking at my chest.

Usually, I'd say something snarky and walk away, but I kind of like the way that he's looking at me right now.

A lot of men look at me the way Ben does. Customers at work, men at the beach, the party boys on my occasional nights out, and even some of the ladies tend to appreciate my appearance. I have been so against getting to know people that my natural state is instant standoffishness.

It's sad to admit that the only person I've ever had sex with was my childhood best friend in the back of his truck. Being so focused on saving money and painting, I've had no desire to even be with a guy, minus the one aborted attempt with Marco.

No desire since...until now apparently. The thought of sex makes me blush, and I think Ben notices.

"I work to fight higher-stakes criminals. Not pretty women who drink a few mai tais on their birthday," he says, interrupting my thoughts. He smiles.

"Don't worry. I'm twenty-one, but you look a little too young to be a lawyer," I say, taking another sip of my drink and returning his judgmental attitude.

"I am. I'll be twenty-six in two months, but I'm very disciplined. I only take the occasional night here and there to get out, and it's even rarer for me to spend time with women," he says flirtatiously.

I'm not sure if that last part is true, based on how his eyes report to every sight of uncovered skin on my body.

"Mm-hmm. Is tonight one those rare nights?" I look away, but curve my lips into a half smile.

Am I flirting right now?

I know he's watching me. I feel his eyes burning a hole through my face, and I'm not sure if it's the drinks or my sudden onset of confidence, but I like it. I like that this particular attractive man finds me desirable.

"Well, my friend Blake has a crush on your friend. So he dragged us all out tonight. Do you not believe that this is rare for me?"

"No, not really." I laugh.

"Why is that?" He smirks.

"Well, obviously you have no issue telling a woman that you find her attractive, which leads me to believe you have had some practice...which is fine. Just be honest about it."

There's my go-to snarkiness.

"Okay, okay," he says, turning his entire body towards me, "I'm a lawyer; I have to be able to persuade. I have clients who pay me big money to use my words, which naturally leaks into other parts of my life."

I'm not sure if his body being closer to mine is making me hot, or if it's the fact that I like his bluntness.

A few guys—I'm assuming Ben's friends—yell over to him, "Ben! We gotta go."

He holds up one of his index fingers to them, mouths, *"One minute,"* and turns back towards me. "Looks like we are heading out; we have an early day tomorrow at the firm."

"It was nice meeting you, Ben," I say, smiling.

He grins back at me. "I know this is forward, but my time is fragile, and I think you are beautiful, so I'm going for it." He pauses. "I'd like to take you out sometime, Penny. I assume you don't have a boyfriend since you've been flirting with me the last fifteen minutes, right?" He pulls his phone out of his pants pocket and hands it to me. "Go ahead and put your number in there."

If this were any other guy tonight telling me to put my number in his phone, I'd tell him to get lost. But I'm feeling drawn to Ben, and it's something I surprisingly want to explore. So I take his phone, input my number, and hand it back to him. "Here you go. And, no, I don't have a boyfriend. I don't even have a cat," I joke.

He laughs. "Good, cats are sketchy. I'll call you. Happy birthday." He takes the tips of my fingers into his hand

and gives them a little squeeze before he goes to catch up with his buddies.

What an odd but extremely enticing gesture.

The tingles that started in my fingertips bolt to my abdomen. I need that physical interaction with a man, need my anatomy to be explored, and need to feel pleased. I don't want to give my heart in any way, just a little piece of my body. Something inside tells me that Ben might just be the one to take it.

I take one more big gulp of my drink and sneak out the back door. I'd rather not explain to Amelia that I'm exhausted and just want to get home. It's about a twenty-minute walk, and it's already kind of late.

Besides, I don't think there could be a better way to end my birthday party.

CHAPTER NINE

By the time I got home, I had a missed call from Amelia, but instead of calling her back, I just sent her a text telling her I wasn't feeling well.

She called another five times until she finally got the message that I was not going to be answering. There was no way I wanted to be persuaded to go back out, and if anyone could guilt me into doing that, it would be Amelia.

I stepped out onto my little balcony that overlooked the pool and saw a couple sitting in the hot tub, cozied up with each other. Either my eyes were playing tricks on me, or the girl was fondling this dude under the water. I didn't judge the couple; in fact, I envied them for having that comfort level with each other. *The world of sex is so foreign to me.*

I grab the little watering can I have stored underneath the end table on my balcony and start to water my plants. Planting flowers in such a little space has proven to be a little difficult, but I've been able to manage a few forget-me-nots and pansies. I have resorted to mostly succulents though. They are still just as beautiful, but a little heartier and less needy. The plants pretty much fill the entire outdoor space, with a few twinkling solar lights here and there.

My balcony has become my favorite place to unwind and read a book or get some painting done. Apparently, on rare occasions, I even see the inappropriate doings of my neighbors.

My phone buzzes in my back pocket. I assume it's Amelia again, but when I look, I see a number I don't recognize.

"Hello?"

"Pen, it's Ben." The voice on the other end of the phone is exactly the one I wanted to hear. "Did you enjoy your party?" he asks instantly.

"I did. I wasn't expecting to hear from you so soon," I admit.

"I don't waste my time." His voice sounds scratchy, as if he's been lying in bed. "People pay me the big bucks for my time, remember?" he jokes.

"Oh yes, that's right. The big-shot lawyer," I say sarcastically.

"Hey, you never know when a lawyer in your back pocket will come in handy." He laughs.

"True."

"You free this weekend?" he asks with no hesitation.

"I work Saturday, but I have the early shift."

"Saturday night, it is." He pauses and then proceeds to say in the sexiest way possible, "I can't wait."

I lean my elbow on the railing. The thought of Ben lying in his bed makes my body warm. I've seen his face and felt his hands, but the rest is left up to my imagination.

Everyone knows how a mind can run wild.

"I'll text you my address," I say, not sure how else to respond to that. If I try to make some flirtatious comment, there's no way it will come out as alluring as his did. So I quickly say goodbye and hang up before I trap myself in a downward spiral of unwanted words.

I replay in my mind what he told me at the party—"I think you are beautiful." It's not the first time I've ever been told this, but for some reason, hearing it from Ben makes me throb in places that don't typically show life.

Realizing I just agreed to a date with a man whom I barely know causes a quick panic attack. *I've never really been on a date,* I think to myself. Unless you count the cheese basket in the back of Myles's truck, or the fiasco at the steakhouse with Marco. I have zero experience with this stuff.

I'm a twenty-one-year-old who has never been on a real fucking date. *How lame am I?*

Chapter Ten

Right about now, I really wish I hadn't returned that tight pink dress. For the last hour, I've been trying to figure out what to wear on my date with Ben. I want to look sexy, but not desperate. Well, maybe a little desperate; there should be no shame in admitting what I want.

I don't have much date-worthy attire, being that my life is waitressing and art. My shirts are either stained with grease or paint—there's really no in-between. I could have tried harder to go out and buy something, but my week got away from me, what with the extra shifts I took at work. Amelia would have lent me something to wear, but I chose to keep this date a secret for now.

I dig deeper into my closet. *There has to be something in here.* I find two dresses. One is black and flowy, with long bell sleeves and dotted with red roses. The other is a plain sage green.

The black one it is.

I've watched countless videos online on how to do a subtle, but desirable, makeup look and haven't been able to master contouring. It should be a class for girls in high school, so we can save ourselves the embarrassment of not blending our makeup perfectly.

I decide to ditch the contouring and put on a thin layer of powder foundation and some eye makeup. If Ben liked how I looked last weekend, then he should like how I look tonight.

I was applying lipstick when I heard a knock on the door. My stomach fluttered with butterflies. I shouldn't be nervous; I have one thing in mind when it comes to Ben, and it shouldn't be too hard to accomplish, but I can't help the nerves that go with uncharted territory.

I quickly do one last mirror check, grab my purse, and open the door to see Ben standing there.

"Good evening, Miss Penny," he says, smiling.

"Hi, Ben." I try to respond with the same flirtatious tone.

"You look very nice," he says as I watch him look at the short length of my dress, which ends at about mid-thigh.

"Thank you."

"These are for you," he says, handing me a bouquet of various yellow and pink flowers.

"They are so pretty. Thank you." I smile and give him a hug. "Let me put them in some water really quick."

I grab a vase from underneath the kitchen sink, fill it with water, and place the flowers in the vase.

"Nice art," Ben says, looking around at the walls. "Who's the painter?"

"I am," I say shyly, not ever having had a man in my apartment before.

"Beautiful," he says, still admiring my work.

I study him for a moment. He's wearing a white button-up shirt with dark-blue jeans, and the smell of his cologne makes me want to crawl on top of him right here and now. He's toned and much taller than I am, which makes me feel as if my femininity stands out.

"Are you ready? Our chariot awaits," he says, gesturing with his hands towards the parking lot.

I lock up my apartment and follow him to his car.

He drives a dark-grey 3 Series BMW; it's fitting for a young, driven lawyer. He walks to the passenger's side of the car and opens the door for me.

Chivalry isn't dead.

The smell of the car almost matches the smell of his cologne.

Ben gets in and turns up the radio just loud enough. "Do you like hip-hop?" he asks, looking at me.

"I don't mind it. I'm more of a blues girl though," I half lie. I really can't stand hip-hop, but I do love the blues.

"An old soul...I like it." He adjusts the volume just a little bit lower. "I'm taking you to the best spot in town. How do you feel about seafood?"

"Honestly, I've really only had salmon and, more recently, lobster," I admit.

"What! Have you been living under a rock?" he jokes.

"Something like that," I say, remembering my processed-foods days.

There are farmers markets on every corner in San Diego, so finding fresh food is pretty easy. I've learned a lot of different ways to prep good foods by just talking to the people who farm their goods. I have yet to dive into the seafood world though. I typically stick with steak and chicken because I know how to cook those. Plus, I do like to support locals. If no one thought of the under-dogs, my art would never sell. I like to believe in good karma—I support the small local fish and hope it comes back full circle, and the big fish will support me.

"So tell me about yourself, Penny," Ben says as we drive to our destination.

"Is there anything in particular that you'd like to know?" *I suck at small talk.*

"Well, I know you're a waitress at the café. Is that what you want to do? Or is there something else that inspires you?"

"Well, clearly I love to paint. I've been doing it for as long as I can remember. It might sound kind of silly, but I honestly just want to live off of my art."

"It's not silly; it sounds like you fit into San Diego quite well." He chuckles and then asks, "Are you from here?"

"I'm from Washington, the northwest side."

"I've never been. Heard it's nice though."

"How about you?"

"Born and raised here."

"Oh yeah? What inspires you?" I ask him with a little smile.

"I get a rush when I win a case. I've been an associate for a while now; they let me take on some of the smaller cases. I've been trying to prove myself, so I work really hard to win."

I can imagine Ben in a nice suit, sitting at a desk and grinding away. It's quite the pleasant image.

"What brought you to the law world?"

"My uncle was a lawyer. I always thought he was the greatest. He had the best suits, the coolest cars, and some really hot girlfriends." He laughs.

I'm not surprised by his comment. So far, Ben's vibe gives off a "dude" image. As if hot chicks and cool cars equal success. Funnily, this doesn't seem to bother me one bit. I have no intention of creating some type of meaningful relationship with him. I've come to the decision that I simply want this man for his body and what it has to offer.

I'm relieved to see that the restaurant isn't super fancy; my dress is nice, but it is not exactly fine-dining material.

The hostess seats us at a table with a view over the water, which is calm tonight.

"Should I order for you?" Ben asks, breaking my attention from the small ripples in the ocean.

"Yeah, that would be great actually," I respond, glancing over the menu quickly.

"Is there anything you won't eat?"

"Oysters look very unappealing to me, so maybe none of those." To me, they look like a shell full of mucus, and I just can't get past that. I don't understand how people eat can eat those.

Ben orders us a plate of buttered scallops and shrimp scampi to share, along with a bottle of their best wine.

I watch him as he sips from his glass. His lips are plump, and his Adam's apple is so prominent, protruding from his neck. I watch as it moves when he swallows.

He catches me staring. "I know looks aren't everything, but it doesn't hurt to have them," he says flirtatiously.

If I weren't so attracted to this man, I would hate that comment, but the burning feeling I get when I think of how our bodies would fit well together takes the animosity out of my reaction.

"I actually find your looks very enticing," I say and then take a slow drink of my wine.

His eyes open wide at my comment, obviously shocked by my bluntness.

I'm shocked by my comment too. *Where did that even come from?*

"Ben, before we get too much further, I need to discuss something with you." I resolve to continue being straightforward and can't believe what I am about to tell him. I don't have experience in speaking to men, especially when I am going to admit what it is I want.

He has a smirk on his face and sits up straight in his seat, giving me his full attention.

"I don't want a relationship or really anything near one. I need something strictly physical," I blurt out and press my lips together. I wince at hearing myself say it out loud.

His smirk turns into a full-out devilish grin. "I'm quite happy to oblige."

I let out the breath I have been holding, and my nerves subside a little.

Thank God.

We eat dinner in silence, but only the silence of words. Our mutual attraction is ear-piercing. The way he eats his pasta is almost seductive. Sucking in the noodles every time one slips away from his mouth. Every few bites, a bit of juice spills onto his lips, and he waits a few seconds before licking it away. I watch his jaw move with every bite and find myself in unfamiliar territory.

Am I seriously turned on by the way Ben eats food? Am I that deprived?

I try to eat my own food, but I feel as if my organs want to jump out of my body. I'm frenzied and need to be touched in ways I've never been.

"Do you want to get out of here?" He says as he drops his fork onto the plate. He seems to have read my mind.

"I really do," I say, taking the napkin off my lap.

He stands up, leaves cash on the table, and takes my hand. We briskly walk back to his car. This time he doesn't open the door for me; he's in a rush to get to our final destination.

"We are going to my place," he demands.

I don't argue because that's exactly what I was hoping would happen.

CHAPTER ELEVEN

Ben's condo is modern; everything matches and is in black and white tones. It's spotless. I wonder if he has a maid who comes in and cleans or if he does it himself. I run my fingers over the entry table as we walk past it—not even a speck of dust. My assumption would be a maid; if he is as busy as he says he is, there is no way he's in here dusting on a weekly basis.

I admire some of the art on the walls. A lot of photography work, mostly of dark mountains and various buildings. Some of the darker images of treetops remind me of the back roads of Washington in the winter.

His place is big enough for a small family; the living room is connected to a large dining area, and the kitchen is larger than my whole apartment. It's such an elegant home; I question if he had an interior designer come in and deck it out for him, but Ben has nice style. It wouldn't surprise me if he was the mastermind.

He tosses his keys on the kitchen counter and stands in front of me. "Do you want a drink?"

"Sure," I say, staring at his lips. If I move a few inches forward, mine will touch his. I half think I should give that a try—why are we postponing something we both want?

I stay patient as he opens a bottle of wine and pours two glasses. I've drunk more wine tonight than ever before; its bitterness does not please my palate, but I can use the liquid courage.

"Are you sure this is all okay?"

"You mean me and you?" I already know what he's referring to, but I want to hear him say it.

"Yeah. Is this a rebound or something? Or do you sincerely not like the whole relationship thing?" He pauses for a second. "Or do you just really want to fuck me?" He grins.

I smile shyly at his comment. I've never had a man say, "Fuck me," to me before.

"It's not a rebound. I just have"—I stop for a second—"like, trust issues or something. Plus, I'm focused on goals. I don't have the time for a relationship." I take a big gulp of my wine. I'm not sure why this conversation makes me so nervous.

"I respect that. I'm focused too," he says and sets his glass on the counter. He walks closer to me, takes my glass, and sets it next to his. There is no hesitation when he grabs me by the waist, pulls me into him, and kisses me hard.

The intensity of his kiss causes electric currents to run through my legs, making me feel weak. I put my hands on the back of his neck for stability. He picks me up, and I wrap my legs around him as he carries me into his room. He tosses me on his black-satin-covered bed, as if I were a piece of laundry, and takes off his shirt.

Of course he has a six-pack.

My heart is nearly beating out of my chest.

"Get undressed," he says sternly.

I do as he says and slip my dress over my head, revealing the black-lace bra and matching panties that I am wearing.

He takes off his pants and climbs on top of me in his boxers. He gives me another strong kiss, but this time his tongue meets mine. They swirl together over and over again. His hand slides behind my bra, unhooks it, and pulls it off my body. He admires my breasts for a second before placing my nipple in his mouth. He sucks gently, and I let out a moan.

My noise must have triggered some kind of animal inside of him because he stands up, yanks off my underwear and then his. Fully naked and erect, he grabs a condom out of his nightstand and puts it on ...and he's back on top of me. He thrusts into me over and over, and I can't help but moan even louder than before. Which only turns him on more and makes him push even harder, sweat profusely, and grunt. Just when I can't hold it back anymore, we both climax. My head flies back, and I let out one last, roaring moan.

"Holy fuck, girl," he says, rolling off me.

Our panting is equally forceful, but it starts to slow as our bodies rest side by side. I can't help but smile. *Damn, this is just what I needed.*

Ben rolls to his side and smirks. "I can get used to this."

"So can I," I admit.

I smell the wine on his breath and admire the dark shade of his eyes. Deep brown, almost as dark as the hair on his chest.

He rolls onto his back and gets up. "I'm going to go shower. You are welcome to stay over if you'd like, or I can take you home when I'm done."

I nod, sit up, and watch his nude body walk into the enormous bathroom. I wait until I hear the water running, and then I get up to find my underwear, which was thrown across the room. I put it back on, along with my bra and dress.

I think Ben and I are on the same page about where we see this going. There's no reason for me to stay. What would that even look like? We go to sleep together and wake up and have breakfast? I can call an Uber and avoid any awkward conversations that may arise with my new FWB. I go into the kitchen and take the last sip of wine in my glass. I find my purse and let myself out.

The air is cooler tonight, and the road is deserted. Ben lives on a cul-de-sac, which eliminates a lot of traffic. Palm trees lit with twinkling lights line both sides of the road. Living an elegant lifestyle doesn't sound terrible, but my heart belongs to the forests.

Which I miss dearly.

CHAPTER TWELVE

Ben texted last night to make sure I got home safely. I assured him that I did, and that was the extent of our conversation until the text I received this morning.

Ben: *Last night was yummy.*

Penny: *It was. I've never had scallops before.*

Ben: *You're funny.*

I respond with a wink emoji, trying to keep the conversation light.

Amelia has a pool day planned for just us girls. I still haven't told her about my rendezvous with Ben, even though I wanted to call her the second I got home. I figured I'd have a chance to spill the tea today. I want to see her facial expression in person since she's been bugging me about dating.

Amelia greets me at the gate to my apartment complex's pool. "Shit, Penny, you look hot in that."

I'm wearing a dark-green bikini with tan beads lining the top. "Ha, thanks."

We make our way to a table shaded by an umbrella and a couple of lounge chairs. "Seriously, have you been working out?" she asks, handing me an ice-cold water bottle.

"Not really." I laugh while taking a drink.

My mind goes back to last night; I guess it could count as a workout. I feel liberated today, more feminine, more womanly. Maybe that is creating an invisible glow that even Amelia, who is 100 percent straight, notices.

"Hold on a sec," she says and grabs my phone. She snaps a picture of me in my bikini. "There, we are putting this on social media. Might get some more followers." She giggles and continues to use my phone.

A few minutes later, she hands it back to me. "That'll do it."

I open my page and see the photo she just took, which is posted at the top, and what she wrote—"Even artists need some fun in the sun."

"Oh my gosh, Amelia, you're ridiculous."

I laugh, but at the same time, I admire my picture. I've come a long way since Port Townsend. Back then, I was confined in a dark hole; my one and only light was Myles. Statistics say I shouldn't be where I am now —thriving in my own skin and living in a safe world over which I have control. I am blossoming into the person I want to be, and my art is following suit.

There are a few things that I carry in my mind. One being that I miss the nature Washington has to offer, specifically in Coupeville. I like San Diego; I enjoy the warm beaches and perfect weather. It has given me the opportunity to build myself and be free. But I fear my heart will always belong elsewhere.

"Penny, did you hear me?" Amelia asks.

I must have fallen so far into a daydream that I hadn't heard her. "Oh, I'm sorry. I was zoned out."

"I said that Blake told me that Ben was into you," she repeats.

"Yeah, I know." I smile.

"Wait! What does that mean?" She jumps up from the lounge chair.

"I wanted to tell you earlier, but I wanted to see how things went first."

"Wait, wait, wait. Please start from the beginning. Did you fuck him?!" She is in fully excited mode right now. I don't blame her; she thinks I'm a prude. Which was somewhat true until now.

"Last night."

"TELL ME EVERYTHING," she demands.

I proceed to tell her almost every detail. What I wore, what he wore, the kind of car he drives. I tell her what we ate and that he ordered us a fancy bottle of wine. I mention his rock-hard abs, and I may have commented on the size of his *undercarriage*.

"I'm so glad you finally have a boyfriend. I was starting to think you were lesbian or something," she taunts.

"Hold on; he's not my boyfriend. We agreed it would just be a physical thing," I correct her.

"Even better." She winks. "Are you going to see him again?"

"Maybe. It was pretty good."

Her jaw drops to the floor. "Who the hell are you?" she jokes. "You are not the Penny I know. But, whoever you are, I like it." She leans back in her lounge chair and soaks in the sun.

It's almost impossible to feel any kind of seasonal blues here; it's pretty much always warm and sunny. I have a good tan going, and the sun has made my hair a bit lighter.

"So who's your flavor of the week?"

Amelia never stays with one guy too long. "His name is Javier," she says, grinning.

"Oh, nice name."

"Yeah, he's okay, I guess. We met at work. He gave me a big tip; plus, he was cute-ish," she says with a shrug.

My phone dings.

I look down, and it's another text from Ben.

Ben: *Hey gorgeous—free tonight? My place—8pm.*

"Is that him?" Amelia glares at me.

"Yes, he wants to meet up again tonight."

"Damn, I guess it WAS that good. Get it, girl." She laughs and shimmies her body in a seductive way.

Penny: *Sounds good.*

As I finish the text, I say to myself, *I think I'll be good at this casual thing.*

Amelia and I spend a few more hours rotating between basking in the sun and cooling off in the pool. After she leaves, I take a shower and scrub my body with my favorite lavender body wash. I put on a red romper and do my makeup. I put on a little extra eyeliner under my eyes to make them a little darker, a little more *romantic*.

Ben lives about fifteen minutes from me, which makes our scandalous visits pretty convenient.

"Hey." He opens the door—shirtless and wearing grey sweatpants.

Oh my gosh.

"Hey" is all I manage to say. I can't take my eyes off his body.

He smiles. "Come in."

I happily obey.

Before I even attempt any kind of small talk to fill the dead space, Ben grabs my hand and leads me to his bedroom. He gently lays me on the bed and starts kissing my neck. He trails from my neck to my cleavage and nibbles just a little bit on my skin.

His gentle movements arouse me, and I want him to be inside of me again. He moves from my chest to my shoulder and down my arm, sending tingling sensations to every place possible. I slide my hand down his back and pull him closer.

I take off my clothes. He takes off his clothes.

Right then and there, he takes me.

After twenty minutes of some serious cardio, he lies next to me. "You sure you're cool with this whole strictly physical thing?"

"I'm sure," I say, resting my eyes.

"Okay, because sometimes girls can get kind of attached and get feelings and all of that."

"Sometimes guys get caught up in feelings too." I turn to him. "If you don't stop asking me if I'm okay with this, I might start thinking you're the one who isn't."

"Nah, I like our setup," he says and gives me a quick kiss on the lips. "We can be friends too, you know. Obviously, I'm attracted to you. And, so far, the sex is fucking great, but we can talk about real stuff too."

I smile. "Yeah, friends sounds good." I get up and get dressed. "I'm going to head home. I'm a little tired after…that."

He laughs. "Let me walk you out."

He walks me to my car, gives me a hug goodbye, and heads back in. I start up my Bronco, turn up the radio, and take the long way home.

I check my mailbox before heading up to my apartment, and I see an envelope bearing my handwritten name—"Penny Wolfe." I open it as soon as I walk in the door. It's a wedding invitation.

You are cordially invited
to witness the marriage of
Whalen Simpkins and Lacey Mower

Lacey Mower—I haven't thought about her in a while. I get a nostalgic feeling just seeing her name.

There is another card in the envelope that lists the date, time, and location of the wedding. As I pull it out, a folded-up note falls out. It's a letter from Lacey.

Penny,

Do you know how hard it was to find your address? You just disappeared into thin air the summer after graduation.

I hope you are doing okay. I honestly thought you were dead for a while, but then I paid the

$3 for an online people search and found your address. I saw your website too. I tried to send an email. So either you are ignoring me, never got my email, or it ended up in the Spam folder. I hope this is even you.

I guess you made your way to Southern California, huh? Lucky girl. I'm still in this rainy state, but IM GETTING MARRIED! Whalen eventually won my heart over. Don't worry; he's matured a lot over the years.

I'd love for you to be there. I know it's the last minute, but only because it took me forever to find you. I know Cali isn't exactly nearby, but if you can get away for a quick visit, that would just make my day so much more special.

There is an art convention going on the same weekend as the wedding. Maybe you can kill two birds with one stone?

Anyways, please give me a call. I'd love to catch up.

Love ya,

She signed her name and included her phone number at the bottom of the note.

I looked at the invite. The wedding was in Seattle in three weeks, and they'd blocked off a whole floor of rooms at the Mayflower Park Hotel.

For the seventeen years I lived in Washington state, I never once made it to Seattle. I always wanted to go see the space needle and check out the art museum, but considering the circumstances I was in, that never happened.

Lacey mentioned an art convention happening the same weekend. I grabbed my phone off the coffee table and started doing some research. I looked for art conventions in Seattle, and one popped up the same weekend as Lacey's wedding. I contemplated it for a few minutes, and ultimately decided that I should go.

I'd love to catch up with my old friend, and it would be very beneficial if I could get a spot at the convention. I could network and showcase my art, and probably price higher too.

I click the link that directs me to the artists' page and fill out the registration form. About five minutes later, I get a confirmation email. *I guess I'm going to Seattle.*

I look at the note Lacey wrote, punch her number into my phone, and give her a call.

Chapter Thirteen

My first time in Seattle was also my first experience on an airplane. The initial bit of turbulence was a little eerie, but I ended up enjoying the bumpy ride. I sat by an older man who told me about a memoir he wrote about his late wife; he was on his way to Seattle to meet a publisher. He had a good sense of humor and was very kind. He even gave me his little bag of complimentary pretzels; he said he was watching his figure and needed to stay carb free. I imagined that was what grandparents were supposed to be like — funny, caring, and generous. He made the flight better than I could have expected.

Work was more than generous in giving me some time off. Probably because I hadn't requested vacation time since I started working there. Lacey's wedding is Saturday, but I flew in Thursday evening so I could get to the convention center early Friday morning. I had a lot of things to set up, and I wanted to make the feng shui perfect. I even ordered some business cards—maroon with white flowers scattered across the top. I liked seeing my name on them.

I feel so professional.

I brought most of my 3-D paintings in which I added real pieces of earth. I think my mom would have loved them. I still think about her often, but I gave up on the hope of ever seeing her again a long time ago. I'm convinced she is dead somewhere. A big part of me hopes that she is, because that would be an easier pill to swallow than the idea of her just not wanting me anymore.

When I get to the hotel, I plop my suitcase on the bed in my room and take out the dress that I'll be wearing to Lacey's wedding. It's long, silky, and yellow. I brought a pair of silver heels to go with it. I hang the dress in the closet so that it doesn't get mixed up with any painting supplies.

The room is gorgeous; it has a big window that overlooks a busy street and the tall buildings downtown. It's sprinkling a little, but a gleam of light shines through a crack in the clouds. It's hard for some people to live in weather that is often gloomy and rainy, but I love it. It brings me back to my old house in Coupeville. When times were blissful.

I often dream of that house. Sometimes I'm there alone, dancing in the living room and out in the back forest. Other times I'm waking up to the smell of breakfast and hear laughter in the kitchen. Perhaps it's a family of my own in there, filling the air with pleasant aromas and noises. Either way, every time I have those dreams, I wake up happy.

My phone buzzes. It's a text from Amelia.

Amelia: Hey, hon, how was the flight?

Penny: Pretty smooth.

Amelia: Miss you already and good luck!

Penny: Thank you. Miss you too!

I walk to the bathroom and look at myself in the mirror. I've gotten more freckles while living in a sunny state, and I kind of like them. I remember my mother's face, so similar to mine. It's probably the only reason why I remember it; I can't escape it. I finger the scar above my right eyebrow; it formed sometime after Grandpa hit my head against the door panel. It's small and only slightly noticeable.

Ben asked about it once; he's the only person who's been close enough to my face to study it in that manner. I told him that I had spooked a cat once, and it clawed at my face. He didn't question it.

I suppose I should be grateful that I don't resemble my grandfather, who I'm not sure is alive or dead at this point. I couldn't care less, to be honest.

I hear some guys running and talking loudly through the hall. They are likely wedding guests because they sound like rowdy twenty-one-year-olds.

It has crossed my mind more than once that Lacey, Whalen, and I have a mutual friend—Myles Ford. I have no clue whether or not they have stayed in touch. Myles was pretty close with them, so I assume they would have invited him to their wedding. After all, they did hunt me down just to send me an invite. Also, the last I knew, Myles was on his way to live in Seattle. Exactly where I am right now.

I have to admit a small part of making the decision to come out here was the hope of running into Myles. I'd love to see how he is doing and to say that I am sorry. He was such a huge part of my life, and I didn't have the guts to tell him that I was leaving.

I wonder if he'd bring someone to the wedding. Maybe he's even married at this point. Twenty-one is kind of a young age to be married, in my opinion, but that didn't stop Lacey and Whalen.

I think of the last day that I saw Myles. Both of our faces overrun by tears and snot, and our hearts overtaken by sadness. A lump forms in my throat, as if

I'm about to cry, when I remember how harsh those feelings were, and the terrible pain that followed.

I shake my head and bring myself back to reality. I need to unpack my enormous portfolio suitcase full of paintings and figure out how I am going to display them tomorrow at the art convention. This is exciting and a big step for me. I'll be exhibiting with other amazing artists in a giant building full of endless creativity.

CHAPTER FOURTEEN

I slept like a baby; this king-size bed is huge in comparison to my full-size one at home. I wish I would have come a day earlier so I could sleep in and lie around in a cozy bed, listening to the raindrops all day. Instead, I'm up by 6:00 a.m. to get down to the convention center and set up. I throw on my black jumpsuit and Converse tennis shoes, put my hair in a ponytail, and load my art into the rental car.

The convention center isn't far from my hotel. It has a huge arch down the middle of it and various plants and statues surrounding it. I'm in awe at how small I feel standing in the middle. Inside there are tall walls separating each artist's spot. The bright lights illuminate every inch and create an inviting ambiance. The voices of artists and hammer clanks echo throughout the space.

I see my name on a sticky note placed on a wall in one of the spaces. A table, a chair, and some easels are already set up for me. There are also adjustable wall hooks, so I can hang some art on the walls as well.

I want to create an inviting appeal, so I lay out my burnt-orange tablecloth and plug in a salt lamp. I even stopped and grabbed some colorful sugar cookies to pass out.

I take a step back, once I'm done setting it all up, and admire how wonderful it all looks. It's amazing to see my own art displayed in such a beautiful way. My pieces are usually just piled up in my apartment or scattered across an old table at an art event.

I'm not one to boast, but I'm proud of myself. I find my cell phone, take a quick picture, and post it to my page. I lay my business cards on the corner of my table and take a seat.

Before too long, I'm up again, networking with people who are interested in my work. I meet a woman from New York—Alice. She tells me this is her favorite art convention in the United States. She comes out every year and purchases one piece. She stays awhile and looks at every single painting I had.

A few photographers came by and took some pictures of a few paintings, and then some of me as well. They asked if they could put it on their website; they update it daily to attract more buyers.

Why would I say no to that?

If I could make enough money to support myself with my art, I would quit Coral's Café in a second. Not that I don't like my job, but how many people get to live out their dreams? Sometimes I imagine myself in my own studio—each wall bears a different mural, and I let aspiring artists come in and use the extra space to work on their own art.

I was just about to head out for the day when Alice came back. "Penny, right?"

"Yes, ma'am."

"Oh please, don't call me ma'am." She waves her hand and walks towards my painting of a naked woman standing in the ocean. The painted sand is covered with real sand, and the ocean is smashed-up larkspur. "I want this one," she says while admiring it.

My eyes go wide. *The ONE piece of art this woman wants to take home, back to New York, is one that I created?*

My armpits start to sweat due to my overwhelmed nerves. "Very good choice," I say, trying to sound confident.

"I was torn between this one and the one over there." She points to the one that lies alone on the main wall.

It was the first 3-D painting I did in San Diego. It took me a while to be able to afford a canvas big enough, but it is my favorite painting. It's a 1990 Chevy Silverado, blue with a white stripe. Parked in a field of flowers in front of a starlit forest. I used light-colored seashells to line the white stripe and the heads of fiddle-necks for the stars.

As I wrap her selection in large pieces of brown paper, then wrap it again in bubble wrap, I think, *I'm secretly glad she didn't pick the truck painting. I'm not sure I really want to sell that one; it holds a special spot in my heart.*

I haven't priced my pieces too high, but maybe I should bump them up a little more because Alice just told me I shouldn't sell myself short when I gave her the total. I did pretty well for a first-timer, I sold two smaller pieces and the large one to Alice.

The staff at the convention center told me that if one of my pieces sells tomorrow while I am gone, they have someone who will take care of it. I guess it's normal for artists to not be there the entire time.

I try to find a good spot to grab dinner afterwards. Seattle is known for their coffee and sea-salted chocolate, but I need something more substantial. I didn't have a chance to eat today because I was so busy socializing, which is great, but now I have a headache due to the lack of nutrition.

I drove around a few minutes before finding a pizza joint that looked pretty good, and it was. The hole-in-the-wall places are usually the best. Before I went back to the hotel, I drive over to the Space Needle. I don't want to go inside because I am so tired, but I admire the exterior of it.

I don't find too much beauty in concrete jungles, but sometimes when the lights hit the buildings at just the right time, they sparkle; there is something mesmerizing about that. It's almost calming, just as a twinkling night-light would be for an infant.

CHAPTER FIFTEEN

The wedding starts at five; it's in the hotel, so I don't have to worry about being late. I went to the original Starbucks this morning for coffee. The letters on the front of the building reminded me of the letters that used to be on the Blockbuster stores. Starbucks isn't my favorite, but while visiting Seattle, it is kind of a "must do."

I stopped in at the convention center to see how things were going. To my surprise, the painting of the truck in the forest was sold. My heart sank a little.

I brought it here in hopes it would draw attention; it was one of my best pieces. I knew while hanging it up that there was a chance it would sell. I guess I just wasn't ready to let it go. But it's gone now, and the only thing I can hope for is that it went to a home that would appreciate it as much as I do.

I take some time to wander around the center to admire others' work. There are a lot of talented people here. One man finds pieces of scrap metal—old clocks, forks, and such—and welds them all together. They are so unique. If I had a big ole house to decorate, I'd consider buying one of his pieces.

I eventually made my way back to the hotel with plenty of time to get ready. I took my time in the shower. Lathered my hair with shampoo and conditioner, shaved my legs, and exfoliated my skin. I feel as if I'm on a mini vacation in this hotel room, so why not pamper myself?

Before getting dressed, I have a few extra minutes, so I call Ben.

"Hey, lady," he says on the third ring. "How's it going out there?" he asks, sounding somewhat busy.

"It's going great. I've already sold multiple pieces," I tell him excitedly.

"Oh, that's awesome."

I can hear people chattering in the background about some case that needs to be looked at immediately. "I'll let you go; you sound busy," I tell him.

"No, it's okay; I just stepped out." But before I can talk more about the convention, he chimes in again, "God, you wouldn't believe what kind of fucking nightmare it is here." I let him tell me about his workload and how some of the associates are just not holding up their end.

"Sorry, I know I'm verbally vomiting on you right now." He chuckles then mumbles something to someone. "Shit, I'm sorry, Penny. I gotta go; let me call you later."

The last few weeks have been exactly what we told each other we were going to be. The sex is great. It's spontaneous and savage and wild. The friendship is good too; we are comfortable enough to call each other and share details about our days.

My support system is odd. My best friend and her parents are my only family, and my only other friend is the guy I am sleeping with. It may be out of the norm, but it works for me, and I'm grateful for every aspect of it.

I put on some light foundation, gold eye shadow, and mascara. I slip on my backless yellow dress and silver heels. I put my hair half up in a sparkly clip and finish my outfit with my favorite accessory, my light-purple flower necklace.

I walk down to the venue and hear light classical music and laughter. A waiter immediately offers me an appetizer and some champagne. I wonder what Whalen and Lacey are doing nowadays to be able to afford this fancy venue and Wagyu hors d'oeuvres. I take a bite of the meat and a sip of the champagne; both hit the spot.

Nice job, Mr. and Mrs. Simpkins.

I make my way around. There are so many unfamiliar faces, and I start to feel incredibly out of place.

I scan the room, desperately trying to spot a familiar face. No sign of Myles, but I do see Julianne sitting at a table with a couple of strangers. I walk over to her.

"Hey, old friend."

Her mouth drops open. "Penny?!" she exclaims and jumps up to hug me. "We all thought you were dead."

"Nope, not dead. I just couldn't stay in Port Townsend anymore. It was time for me to go. I'm sorry I didn't say goodbye," I tell her, hugging her back.

"Don't be sorry. It's better to rip the Band-Aid off anyways."

That was exactly my thought all those years ago.

We catch up; she asks me how I've been doing. I show her my art page and tell her about the convention. I ask how it's going in New York, and she seems to love it there. She is getting her master's in public health, so she has to head back right away in the morning.

We end up bumping into Justin and his new girlfriend and some other old classmates.

The ceremony was beautiful. They got married under twinkling lights, surrounded by beautiful flower arrangements. She chose light pink and sage green for her colors—I take mental notes because I plan to paint them something related to their wedding as a gift. Lacey looked amazing in her mermaid-style dress and pearls in her hair. Whalen had gained a few pounds, but he needed it; he was always so scrawny. More importantly, they both looked incredibly happy.

"Penny! I am so happy to see you!" Lacey greets me at the reception.

"Congrats, you guys! It's so good to see you too." I give her and Whalen a hug.

"Babe, have you seen Justin anywhere?" Whalen asks Lacey.

She ignores him and points over to the bar.

"Thanks for coming. I'm glad you're not at the bottom of the ocean or something," Whalen says to me and walks off to find his twin.

"So tell me the juice! What's new? How's California? Dating anyone?"

We sit down at a table together, and I give her the lowdown. "California's great; it's sunny and warm and has some pretty good food too. And I guess I am kind of seeing someone, but it's nothing serious. It's more of a friends-with-benefits thing."

"Oh, sounds saucy." She giggles. "And what about Myles? You guys were joined at the hip."

Her question makes me think that she hasn't talked to him either—meaning, he probably won't be here. "We drifted apart; you know how that goes," I admit.

"Well, Whalen sent him an invite, but we never got a response. They haven't spoken much this past year. Whalen travels a lot for work, so outside of Justin, he's kind of a hermit." She shrugs. "Anyways, I need to go mingle. I'm sincerely happy that you came today, Penny; it means the world to me." She gives me another hug and makes her way to the next table.

Oof, I need a real drink.

I head over to the bar. "Can I get a Vodka Cranberry, please?" I ask the bartender.

He asks to see my ID and goes to make my drink.

The bar is dark wood accessorized with baby's breath hanging from small ropes. I love the look of it and think I may add some to my balcony when I get back home. Baby's breath is underrated—so delicate and pure.

"Penelope Wolfe?"

I hear my name. My entire body stiffens, and my heart races. I know that voice. No one but the owner of that voice can so simply say my name and make my entire body aware of every throb.

Myles.

Everything you could imagine a perfect man looking like is what he is. Tall with broad shoulders. His muscles are barely contained inside of his tight button-up shirt. His sandy-blond hair still rests just over his baby-blue eyes. Even his jaw looks stronger.

I look at him, and his eyes are staring directly into mine. I'm not sure what to say in this moment. *Do I slap him across the face and release the anger left over from his leaving me all alone? Do I immediately apologize for disappearing?*

"Myles, hi," is what I manage to deliver.

He slowly comes closer to me. His right hand reaches over my left side and behind me, but he doesn't touch me. Instead, he hands me my drink, which is sitting on the bar. His eyes stray from mine; he looks at my neck and notices my necklace, the one he gave me for my eighteenth birthday. The only piece of jewelry I have ever cherished.

"I always liked you in yellow." He smiles slightly and takes a seat at the bar.

I join him.

"How are you?" I ask, taking a slow sip of my drink. "Are you chief yet?" *Here I am, confronted with stupid small talk again.*

"Ha, no. I have some time before that, but I am working on being a lieutenant soon," he says as the bartender brings him a beer. "How about you? Are you rich and famous?" he asks and takes a gulp.

"Oh, I wish. I still drive my old Bronco." I awkwardly chuckle.

He doesn't laugh with me. Instead, he looks at me, his face stern. "Where have you been?"

I sigh quietly and answer, "San Diego." I can't look him in the eyes. I couldn't bear to see an ounce of pain and be okay with it right now. Guilt overruns me.

"How do you like it out there?" He looks away, breaking the painful silence.

"It's nice and warm. Are you still here in Seattle?" I ask him and quickly finish the rest of my drink.

"I am," he says stoically.

When I received Lacey's wedding invitation, I had run through this encounter a few times in my head. Each time, I felt the exact way I am feeling right now — stiff and bumbling over my words.

Before either of us has a chance to continue the conversation, Justin and Whalen come over and put Myles in a playful headlock. "What's up, bro? Where the fuck have you been?" Justin asks, slightly slurring his words.

"I've been around. I wouldn't have missed your wedding," Myles says, breaking out of the headlock.

"I see you two are still friends." Whalen nods towards me and puts the word *friends* in finger quotation marks.

"I'm surprised we didn't go to your wedding first," Justin chimes in.

Myles let's out an awkward laugh.

My face turns bright red, and as much as I'd love to sit here with him, I am very aware of how uncomfortable I am. I need to talk to him, but alone and with no distractions. Before I slip away, I reach over the bar and grab a napkin. I take a pen from my wristlet, write a note, and slide it over to Myles.

Room 302—just knock 3 times.

Chapter Sixteen

I've been sitting on the edge of my bed for almost an hour. I had another drink with Julianne and said my last congratulations to Lacey and Whalen before I went back up to my room. I'm not anywhere near satisfied with how my conversation went with Myles, so I'm really hoping he shows up. I need to talk to him privately, with no distractions, no alcohol, and no drunk friends who want to catch up.

I figure an hour is a long enough time to wait, so I take off my dress and put on an oversized T-shirt. I can't blame him for not wanting to talk to me; I didn't give him the decency of explaining or apologizing years ago. I could have dug harder to find contact information for him, as Lacey did to send me her wedding invite.

Although, he could have done the same to find me.

I suppose that part of my life is over for good now. Myles was what he was supposed to be for me—my childhood best friend, my first kiss, and my first love. This could be the closure we both need.

Knock, knock, knock.

My heart skips a beat. *I spoke too soon.*

I open the door and see him standing tall, his suit coat draped over one arm.

"Come in," I say with a flushed face. *This probably looks bad. I'm standing here in just a T-shirt after inviting the man I lost my virginity to into my hotel room.* My intentions are only pure, but it's hard to stay completely innocent-minded when a man like Myles Ford is standing in front me.

He walks in, lays his coat over one the chairs, and turns to face me. "Why didn't you call, Penny? What happened? Did you hate me for leaving and feel the need to punish me?" His eyes quickly move back and forth between mine.

"Myles, no, of course not." I pause for a second before confessing, "I had to leave; he was going to end up killing me." I sit sadly on the bed.

He stands for a few seconds longer; slumps his shoulders, then sits with me. "I thought he had stopped doing that." He looks down at his hands.

"It got better. But, that day you left, he saw me hugging you, and he lost it. He said such terrible things and — well, it was the last time I was going to take it," I said. "You were gone. I had no reason to stay."

Myles put his right hand over my left. "I should have stayed with you," he whispers.

I look up at him. "No, Myles. You did the right thing. There was no future for you in Port Townsend; there was no future for me there either. We both had to leave. I hope you will forgive me for how it happened. At the time, I thought the best thing was to cut all ties...including with you." I wince, hoping he will find forgiveness.

His eyes meet mine and then make their way to my scar. He grazes it with his finger; his gentle touch feels perfect on my skin. "I understand," he says and takes his hand away.

"Are you still painting?" he asks, adjusting his position to be more comfortable.

"I am." I perk up a little. "In fact, I have a spot at the art convention here, and I've sold some pieces. People seem to really like my work."

"Yeah? Tell me more."

We sit cross-legged facing each other, like little kids. I tell him all about my work, how I add pieces of nature to my paintings. I tell him about the lady from New York and that if I can sell enough pieces, I plan to quit waitressing and live off what I make.

We talk about his time in the academy and how he was top of his class. He tells me some stories of a few calls he has been on and that being a firefighter is one of the most rewarding things he has ever experienced.

I tell him about my time being homeless and living in my car and that I have a new friend named Amelia. I reminisce about the mornings I woke up parked next to a beach and could hear the waves crashing on the shore. He tells me he hasn't traveled and that he'd love to visit California one day.

I don't tell him about Ben. Not that I was trying to hide it—or maybe subconsciously I was—but Ben didn't even cross my mind while I was sitting with Myles. Talking to him brought back every nostalgic and happy feeling I ever felt. It's almost as if we slipped back into exactly where we left off.

"Whoa, it's after 3:00 a.m.," I say, looking at the clock.

"Damn, I should get out of here," he says, shuffling his feet.

"How far do you live?"

"About thirty minutes, not too far. I'm off tomorrow, so I'm not worried about it."

If I were going to listen to my heart, I'd invite him to stay over and plan an entire day together tomorrow. But based on these emotions floating in the air around us, I already know where that would lead, and I don't think either one of us would know how to handle that.

We both scoot off the bed and stand up. My chest bumps into his, and we are face-to-face. His breathing goes from calm to shaky, and I can feel my heart racing. His hands slowly move up from his sides and onto my waist. I follow suit and place my hands up on his shoulders. He looks me in the eyes.

I could just melt.

I love those beautiful blue eyes. His head moves slowly closer to mine...until our lips slightly touch. He pulls me a little closer, and his lips press a little harder against mine.

This kiss is heaven.

I'm numb, and I have lost all sense of reality. There is no Earth, no moon, and no stars. Cars, houses, and shopping malls are all gone. Sirens and church bells have silenced across the globe. Nothing exists...except me, Myles, and the grasp we have on each other.

We slowly pull away, and reality smacks down on us. He lets go of me and starts walking towards the door; then he stops and turns around.

"Thank you, Penny. I needed this. Take care," he says. He places a piece of paper on the counter closest to him and leaves.

When the door closes, I pick up the paper. It's my note from earlier. I turn it over and smile at his handwriting, remembering the days we passed notes back and forth between our houses. I smile even more at the words written—

I'll always be here for you.

The next morning I am up early again and heading to the convention center to pack up. I never even fell asleep, so I guess, technically, I've been up since yesterday morning. I couldn't stop my mind from running through my night with Myles and every moment we have shared together since we were eleven. I felt so incredibly grateful that I had someone like him in my life. He kept me alive. Motivated. Inspired. He made me happy.

My heart hurts in both good and bad ways. I'm glad that I was able to explain what happened and that we were able to fill each other in on the years we have missed. His words, *"Take care,"* play over and over in my head. I'm conflicted.

If the tables were turned, and Myles had disappeared, I would have probably wanted to die. I was already broken, and he was all I had. He came from so much more; his foundation was strong with a mother who loved him and a father who taught him how to be a man.

His roots are healthy and buried in a family plot full of life and love. Mine are sick in a field of loss and sorrow.

My hope is to have learned a thing or two from Myles about what a happy heart can be and to create a new set of roots. Ones that are formed with a hard exterior. Crystalized stone. Filled with a radiating warmth that soothes every emotional scrape and bruise. Filled with unconditional love that only leaves healthy soil behind for new bountiful roots to fill.

I want to break the chain.

CHAPTER SEVENTEEN

I sold three more pieces at the convention, seven in total. I also had a lot of people take my business card. They asked if I shipped my art, and I happily reassured them that I sure did. In fact, I already had five inquiries in my email.

When I returned to San Diego, I was greeted by a flower delivery. They were addressed to Ms. Penny Wolfe. I hurried to open the card.

I've missed your body.
Ben

I shouldn't have been disappointed to see Ben's name there, but I was. I wasn't expecting flowers from Myles, or anything at all from him, but as soon as I saw the flowers sitting on my doorstep, my mind went to Myles. Flowers were our thing.

I bring in the bouquet of sunflowers and set them on the counter. I drop my suitcase and art carriers right in the middle of the floor and take out my phone.

Penny: Thank you for the flowers. They are beautiful!

A few minutes later, my phone dings.

Ben: Glad you like them. I'm done for the night. Can I come by?

He arrives about twenty minutes later and greets me with a kiss on the cheek. "How was your trip?"

"It was great. I sold a bunch of work."

He helps me unload my artwork and places the canvases against the wall next to my bed.

"I should probably shower; airplanes make me feel icky."

I say see a smirk grow on Ben's face as soon as I mention the shower. I guess my words were an invitation, but for the first time since knowing Ben, I didn't crave him as he was craving me. Which I'm almost certain has everything to do with seeing Myles. I just want to go sit in the shower and let the hot water fall over me.

However, I don't want to disappoint Ben, so I nod my head towards the shower and confirm the invitation. I take off my clothes; Ben copies me. I'm the first one in, and a few seconds later he's with me.

We start kissing immediately; almost instantly after that, his fingers are inside of me. I can't help but let out a moan. Ben is good with his hands, and now that we have spent intimate time together, he knows how to get me going. He continues to finger me until he gets so overwhelmed with lust that he pulls his fingers out and drives himself inside of me.

He's hard and fast. He doesn't stop to readjust as our bodies are sliding around the shower. The only thing on his mind is thrusting in and out as fast as he can. The hot water mixed with the cardio are almost too much. After what seems like forty-five minutes, he pulls out and finishes on the shower floor.

I am completely out of breath and am not sure if I got cleaner or dirtier during this shower.

Ben quickly suds himself up and rinses off. "Yum, I'll meet you out there." He winks and hops out.

I think about Myles for a second and what sex in the shower would be like with him. Is it wrong for me to think of him when I'm with Ben? The ethical part of me feels as if I should disclose my feelings for Myles. Even though my relationship with Ben would technically be classified as fuck buddies, Ben is also a friend now; it almost feels as if I'm emotionally cheating on him.

I dry off and put on a robe.

Ben sticks his head in. "I'm hungry; let's order Chinese," he suggests.

Chinese food sounds amazing right now. "Sounds great."

"Hey, Penny?" Ben looks at me and smiles.

I turn to acknowledge him.

"I adore fucking you." His head disappears, and I hear his feet shuffle into the kitchen.

His words make my face warm. I don't know if I'll ever get used to him—or any man, really—saying that to me. I finish up and meet him in the kitchen.

"It'll be here in a half hour; here's some water," Ben says, sliding a water bottle down the counter.

"Thank you." I take a few gulps and contemplate my next words. "Ben, I feel like there is something I need to tell you." I sit down at the table. "Do you remember my childhood best friend I told you about?"

"Yeah, the guy?"

"Yes, his name is Myles."

Ben nods as he remembers the conversation we had a couple of weeks ago after a quickie on his couch.

"I ran into him at the wedding," I mumble.

"You're in love with him, aren't you?"

His words shock me. *Is it that obvious?*

"I did love him. We haven't talked or seen each other since we were seventeen. When I saw him at the wedding, all these old feelings rushed back."

I turn to look at Ben; he looks a little surprised, but not upset.

"I know exactly how you feel, Penny," he says and sits down at the table.

"You do?" I ask.

"Yeah, I do. There was this girl in college that I fell head over heels for, like movie-type love. I was crazy about her, and she was crazy about me. Her name is Sophia, and we were inseparable. When we graduated college, she went to another school for an extended specialty-nursing program. We tried to do the long-distance thing, but eventually it got to be too much, so we broke up. I was devastated, but time helped with the pain."

He stops for a second and sighs. "I waited for her. I didn't date anyone. I mean, I hooked up with some girls, but nothing even remotely near serious. I found out about six months ago that she got engaged." Ben half smiles at me. "She is my Myles."

My heart drops, and I admire Ben for his vulnerability. "I'm so sorry, Ben," I say, resting my hand on top of his.

"Don't be sorry; it's just how things go," he says, finishing off his water bottle. "I can't say I'm super excited to hear you have feelings for someone…only because it may interfere with what we have going"—he pauses—"which has been really great, in my opinion." He winks. "Is Myles with anyone?"

"I don't know, to be honest, but he did kiss me."

"Ah, his feelings are mutual," Ben says and smiles. "Look, you and I fill each other's sexual needs, and I'd love to keep doing that for as long as it makes sense, but I also care about you beyond that. You're a good person, Penny, and if there is even a possibility that this could work between you two, why not take the chance?"

I like this version of Ben.

"If Sophia came knocking on my door, I'd drop everything…and everyone…for her. That's what true love is," he says, pulling me in for a hug. "Why not go for it?"

I've run that question through my mind a million times in the last twenty-four hours. "My life is here, and his is in Seattle." I look down at the floor.

"You never know what can happen. Keep your mind open to the possibilities," he says and smiles.

The doorbell rings.

"Let's eat."

Chapter Eighteen

It's been a month since my trip to Seattle. The initial excitement over the increased interest in my artwork has turned into anxiety over the serious workload. I've got another five orders in my inbox, and I wasn't even finished with the first five. Perfection takes time.

I've thought a lot about what a relationship with Myles would look like. I couldn't be with him and live here at the same time. I've finally found a stable environment, and I'm terrified about uprooting myself from it. At the same time, I wouldn't ask him to leave his life and everything he has worked so hard to accomplish. I know he wouldn't ask that of me either…assuming he would even want a relationship with me at this point. I keep repeating to myself what Ben said, *You never know what could happen.* Even though I agree with that statement, I'm leaving it up to the universe.

Amelia invited me out for some coffee and a walk this morning. She told me there was something I needed to see. After we ordered our iced lattes, she walked me down the street and stopped at a building. It was an art studio.

"He rents it out on the weekends for people to show-case their art," she says, opening her arms towards the building. "Let's go in." She opens the door.

The space had high ceilings and one window facing the street; it took up almost the entire wall. *Perfect to showcase artwork.* The walls were painted a light blue, and the floor was a sandy tan; it matched the beachy vibe of the town.

"Hey, Amelia," the guy in the back says, walking towards her. "Is this your friend you were talking about?" He points to me.

"Yes, this is Penny. She's the artist."

The man holds out his hand for a handshake. "Hi, Penny. I'm Scott."

I shake his hand. "Hi, is this your place?" He looks pretty young to own this studio.

"Nah, it's my dad's. You can see that it's mostly empty. He travels a lot and only uses it when he's around. He rents it out to people who need a space for a night or two."

I take a walk around the studio, admiring the way that some shelves are uniquely placed.

"I met Scott at work last week," Amelia says, following me. "He told me about this place, and I just had to show you. We could throw an art party here."

I'm not sure that I would call it an art party, but it's a brilliant idea. I could put some serious work into networking and make it a big event. "That's not a bad idea."

"It's booked out for a bit, but we could get your name on the list. I can send you an email with all of the pricing and details if you'd like," Scott chimes in.

"That would be great! Thank you, Scott."

"Don't thank me. Thank Amelia. She's, uh...pretty persuasive." He chuckles.

Okay, that makes a lot more sense. Scott was pretty cute; there's no way Amelia would have passed him up.

I give him my email and phone number. Amelia gives him a quick peck on the lips and promises to see him later.

I had signed up to attend a local art show that afternoon. So, before leaving, I told Scott that if he and/or his dad were around, they should check it out. If Scott's dad is a known artist locally, it might be a good idea to get to know him a little bit; maybe he could get me some more attendees for my art party.

"That was awesome," I say to Amelia as we leave.

"I knew you'd be excited. We could advertise at work. I bet all your regulars would love to come see your art."

"You are just full of amazing ideas today," I say, giving her a little side hug.

"Let's head back; you have to get to your event," she says, hugging me back.

I parked on a side street and had to make two trips to grab all my artwork, which is why I'm now a sweaty mess.

I had my own E-Z UP, a table, and a chair. I brought two easels to set in front of the E-Z UP. I put two of my newer pieces on them and then a few smaller pieces on the table. I leaned the rest of the larger pieces against the front of the E-Z UP.

I don't plan to sell all of these; I'd be lucky to sell one, but the placement of them is key. You need the ones that grab attention out front, and the smaller and more affordable artwork behind them. It's some kind of mind game people play with themselves to justify a purchase.

Ben said he would try to stop by, but he has been working all day and night on a case. I don't think he even went to sleep last night. We see each other on a weekly basis, but it's starting to feel less and less satisfying. Not that I'm not attracted to him, but my heart hasn't been in it; our relationship now has an odd vibe to it. I'm more interested in Ben as a friend at this point. Some of that must be because I left my heart with Myles in Seattle.

I think Ben feels the same; bringing up Sophia has put him in a funk. He showed me pictures of her the last time we were together, and you could just feel the ache in his heart.

Like me, he left his heart with Sophia.

There are more people here than I expected there to be, and many of them stopped to admire my work. I sold a painting of a single pink rose, made with rose petals, to a guy who was looking for an anniversary gift. He told me his wife's favorite color was pink, and her favorite flower was a rose. He was a fisherman visiting San Diego to get some new gear for his boat. He was supposed to miss his anniversary, but he decided to head home early and surprise his wife with a gift. I admired the tattoo of a mermaid on his forearm and wondered about the story behind it, besides his obvious love for his wife.

"This won't die, like a bouquet of flowers will," he told me when he picked the piece up to study it. "Don't worry. I'm still getting the real flowers too," he quickly added and laughed.

"Smart man," I say, wrapping the painting.

As the man walked away, Amelia was walking towards me with a brown paper bag. "I thought you'd be busy and probably hungry, so I brought you a sandwich from work," she said, handing me the bag.

"Oh, thank you so much. I'm starving." I take the sandwich out of the bag and shove almost half of it in my mouth.

"Is this practice for Ben?" she jokes. "Just kidding. I have to get back to work in a few, but I wanted to check in on you and see how you were doing." She smiles.

"You're such a good friend. Thank you, Amelia." I give her a hug before she's on her way.

After lunchtime, the crowd starts to die down. I sold just the one piece today, but a lot of people have taken my business card. So I'd count today as a win. I start to wrap up some of the bigger pieces. I'm going to try to get a head start and beat some of the exiting traffic.

"Is that a dahlia?"

I freeze when I hear a woman's voice. I know that voice. I'm not sure where I know it from, but somewhere in the depths of my brain, I know it. It feels as if electric ice is running through my veins and keeping me frozen in my exact posture. My feet feel heavy, as if they are filled with emotional concrete.

Peaceful, graceful, and delicate, her words are. *How do I know that voice?*

It seems as if minutes have passed before I am able to regain the strength needed to move my body towards what I fear is a ghost. I'm terrified of whom I'll be facing when I turn around. I force myself to move because the thought of losing out on this moment is even more terrifying than embracing it.

As I slowly pivot…there I stand…face-to-face with Ms. Iris Wolfe…my mother.

I stare at her. She stares at me. The shock I feel in my bones doesn't seem to match her calm affect.

"Penelope, these are beautiful," she says, lightly touching the painting closest to her, "and so are you."

I'm still speechless. I look more like her than I thought I did. She shows signs of aging, but it has only made her more beautiful. I'm confused and angry and relieved, all at once. She's alive, and she's here, standing right in front of me.

"I'm sure you have a lot of questions," she says gently. "I'd love for us to sit down and talk."

Sit down and talk? Like we are old friends catching up? What the fuck is wrong with this woman?

I don't know how to speak right now. I seem to have forgotten all of my words. My face muscles are paralyzed, and I don't know if this is even real.

Did I trip on something and face-plant into the concrete? Am I dead? Is this heaven? Hell?!

Interrupting my neurotic thoughts, she says, "I know this is a lot," as she looks at me intensely. "How about we plan to meet later instead?" she asks, nearly whispering. "Just gather your thoughts"—she takes one of my business cards—"and I'll call you a little later." She walks away and catches up to a stalky man. Her long, red-floral dress nearly drags on the ground.

Did I just see a ghost?

"Um, are you okay?" the vendor next to me asks as she packs up her handmade journals.

I look over at her. "Did a woman just come here and talk to me?" I ask while trying to wake up from this daze.

"Yeah, she looked just like you," she says confidently.

Okay, this is real. My mother, the woman I ached for, for years and years, was really just here. She is the reason I cried myself to sleep so many nights. She is the person who brought love to my world and so quickly ripped it away from me. She is the first person to ever break my heart.

My mother was here, within arm's reach, and I didn't budge. That realization hits me like a train, and I run in the direction she went. I twirl around to try to find her. I look to my left, and then to my right. I shield my eyes from the setting sun and look in every possible crevice of the world around me.

No sight of her. I stand there for a minute and close my eyes.

I don't believe in God. If there were a higher being who loved all His children, He wouldn't have put me through what I went through. But in this moment...just in case I'm wrong and there is a God out there...I pray.

Please send her back to me. Please have her call me. Please give me another chance...just one more chance.

When I open my eyes, nothing has changed. People still surround me. I hear the chatter and noises of people packing up and driving away. I shake my head to try to ground myself. I take a deep breath of air and head back to my booth to pack up.

And anxiously wait for whatever happens next.

Chapter Nineteen

It's been three hours since I left the art event. I've been pacing back and forth in my apartment since the second I walked in. I even ignored Ben's call on the off chance that it would somehow interfere with my mother's phone call.

How did I let her just walk away? I'm such an idiot.

I wait another hour. My legs grow tired, and my pacing turns into lying face down on my bed. My phone is right next to me, the ringer set to the loudest volume, which makes my heart jump when it finally sounds off. I look down at my phone and see an unknown number.

Oh my God.

I quickly answer, "Hello?" My breath is shaky.

"Penelope, hi."

It's her. She has the same calming voice as she did hours ago.

"Hi." *Do I say Mom? Iris? What is she to me? What am I to her?*

"I'm sorry about earlier. I know my appearance must have come as a surprise," she says, "but I knew this day would come. We have so much to talk about."

"Um, yeah, we do," I say, not sure how to approach this. She is a complete stranger to me.

"Are you free tomorrow morning? Let's talk in person. I can meet you for coffee. Just the two of us," she says.

I remember the stalky man she walked away with. *Is she saying this to tell me that she won't be bringing him? Or so I won't bring someone?*

"Yes, I'm available." *This sounds more like an interview than coffee with my long-lost mother.*

"Okay, meet me at Grassroots Café. Let's say 9:00 a.m.?" She's whispering again.

"I'll be there."

She says goodbye, and I hang up.

I drop my phone onto my bed and go to look in the mirror. I study my face and compare it to hers. We are nearly identical, except for our noses. I must have inherited that from my dad.

I think about him. He couldn't have been the stalky man; there was absolutely no resemblance.

I have so many questions for her. I grab my journal off my nightstand and start writing everything that is running through my mind. It races faster than my hand could ever follow. Half of the scribbles are not legible; the others are carefully written when I have something more important to remember or ask.

I feel so incredibly lonely. The way I used to feel when I was a child. Before I met Myles, anyway.

I think of him too. I don't want to confide in Ben; he wouldn't understand. Amelia is sweet, but almost too optimistic for this one. There is only one person on this planet with whom I'd care to share this moment—that is, of course, Myles.

I feel a pain in my abdomen and realize just how much I miss him. The sudden shock of seeing my mother after all of these years has drained me. I feel as if I have just been physically attacked and sucked dry by some mystical beast. It reminds me of the days when Grandpa hurt me.

I always turned to Myles in those dark times, and he never once made me feel bad about needing him. His presence alone was healing.

I had put in my nightstand, next to my bed, the note he left me in my hotel room that night. I take it out now and hold it to my chest. I wonder what he's doing at this very moment.

Does he think about me as much as I think about him?

CHAPTER TWENTY

I've been up since five this morning. I couldn't sleep well;
every single possible thought ran through my mind.

What do I even wear?

I want to present myself in a way that Mom would be
proud of me. I want her to see how far I've come and
that I have done it all alone. At the same time, I want
her to feel guilty. I want to look into her eyes and see
what she feels deep down inside when I tell her she left
me with a man who could have killed me.

What would that outfit look like?

I picked a pair of boot-cut jeans and a lavender
tank top with a black, fedora-style hat—sophisticated
but stylish.

I'm fifteen minutes early to Grassroots Café. It's a small coffee/bakery shop with only outdoor seating. I see my mother already sitting in a spot, two cups in front of her.

She's early too. I wonder if she's as nervous as I am.

I haven't built up the courage to get out of my car and go sit with her. I don't think I have been more scared in all my life. Not even when I came home and noticed that Grandpa was drunk. No physical pain could ever amount to the emotional pain this woman has put me through.

I have so many questions for her. To some, I don't necessarily want answers. I question whether or not I should just go back home and try to pretend that none of this ever happened. However, the little girl in me needs this, and I want to give that to her. So I force myself out of the car and walk to her, my legs shaking with every step.

You got this, Penny.

I startle Mom when I abruptly sit down in front of her, trying to extrude any ounce of confidence I have.

"Oh, hi. Here, I got you the lavender tea. They said it's their most popular," Mom says, sliding a hot cup over to me.

"Thank you." I take a sip. It's not the most terrible drink I've had, but it's definitely not something I would have picked for myself.

"So you're an artist now? Your work is beautiful."

"Well, it's kind of a second job for now. I'm a waitress."

She smiles and nods. "When did you end up out here?"

"I was seventeen."

This information doesn't shock her. In fact, she's almost emotionless.

"I see," she says and takes a drink of her tea. "Oof, this isn't so good," she admits, which makes me smile. There is some kind of normalcy in the weirdness of this all.

"Penny, we have so much to talk about. Should I start? Or would you like to?"

I'm grateful that she gave me that option. I'd much rather that she explain herself first. I think it will give me some time to release some of these butterflies and finally see that she is a person, not a spirit who is haunting me.

"You first."

"Okay. Well, I remember you as a little girl so clearly. I collect memories of your rosy cheeks and beautiful smile. I loved how you admired nature just as much as I did. I hope, after today, you will understand why I had to go." She stops and takes another sip.

"I had this dream two nights before the last day I saw you. I was in hell, there was fire, and I was at war, trying to protect you from the evils of this world. I started hearing voices. Your grandma and grandpa thought I was crazy, but the voices told me I had to find the center of this demonic being. I realized I had to leave, or else the demons would find you and take you away from me. I had to remove myself so they could never find you."

My eyes widen. *Is this some kind of a joke to her?*

"Penny, I found it. I found the balance that those voices wanted and sacrificed myself for years. They knew I was in such grave pain from being separated from you, and that is what they wanted all along. After some time, the voices diminished. Whatever I did, it worked because here you are, sitting in front of me in the flesh; you're safe. Now you and I can be together again." She shows emotion now; tears are starting to form in her eyes. "I knew this day would come."

"What the hell are you talking about?" I start to get angry. "You know what? Never mind. This was a huge mistake." I stand up to leave, but hear a shout from across the street.

175

"Hey!" the stalky man from yesterday yells and comes running over to us. "Iris, what are you doing here?" He seems concerned.

"I'm so sorry, Miss. She really shouldn't be out and about alone," he says, holding my mother's hands.

"Otis, I'm fine. This is my daughter," she says, nodding towards me.

"You are her daughter?" he asks confusedly.

I nod, just as confused as he is.

"Iris, we need to get back now," he says gently to Mom.

She shakes her head and starts squirming in his grasp.

"Leave her alone," I say defensively, ready to push him away.

"I know how this looks, but you don't understand. She's a patient." He pulls up my mother's right sleeve and reveals an ID band around her wrist.

A patient? She's crazy?

"Look, we really need to get her back. It's been hours since she's had her medication. Iris, honey, why don't we invite Penny back with us." He handles her so kindly and patiently, and his suggestion brings light to her eyes.

"Oh, what a wonderful idea," Mom says, jumping with glee. "Would you please come?"

I stare at her and feel the world around me shatter a little bit. I look at Otis. My mother and he are patiently waiting and pleadingly looking at me for an answer.

"Do you want to meet us at the South Sweet Recovery Center?" he asks. "I can explain everything. In fact, I'm glad this happened. We haven't been able to locate any of Iris's relatives."

The fact that my mother is clinically crazy crushes me. At the same time, it's bittersweet. This whole time, I thought she didn't love me. But in her own reality, that's the only reason why she left—because she loves me. I think of the pain she must have felt. But, then again, did she feel pain? Or did the psychotic thoughts mask it?

I need answers, so I say yes.

He hands me a card that has his name and the address of the center to where they are going.

Otis Hopkins
South Sweet Recovery Center

"See you soon, Penny!" my mom squeals before leaving with Otis.

Processing everything that just happened in the last twenty minutes seems impossible. I let myself cry right there, in the middle of the patio, for other patrons to witness. I cry for the little girl who felt she wasn't wanted by her mother...and for the teenager who had to experience hormonal and body changes all alone. I cry for the woman who had to learn how to be feminine and graceful through trial and error. I cry for my mother, whose brain is sickened with intrusive thoughts that create an extremely false reality.

It makes sense now. I remember her talking about the fairies in the forest and how they talked to her and told her how lovely we were. I recall Grandpa yelling at my mother in the middle of the night, saying that she was a lunatic for believing in the world the way she did.

I wonder if Grandpa was the demonic being from which she was running. If he was able to hurt me, he probably did the same to my mom when she was young. Maybe she created an alternate reality and subconsciously created the voices in her head. Maybe she got in too deep and couldn't crawl back out. Everyone has their own ways of dealing with trauma; perhaps that was her way.

All I know now is that this is the reality now—I believe she needs me as much as I need her.

I sit in the waiting room after filling out some paperwork. The number of questions on that clipboard is obnoxious—half of them I didn't know how to answer. It's hard to disclose information about your own mental-health history when you're not exactly sure what's up and what's down.

Obviously, my mother is ill. Who knows about my father? Either my own mental demise is dormant, or I got lucky. *Then again, crazy people don't know that they are crazy.*

I see Otis making his way to me. "Your mom is okay. Apparently, she walked right on out of here when another patient was checking out. She took a bus to go and meet you. Do you want to come on back with me? I think we should chat, and then you can visit with your mom. She's resting right now while the meds kick in."

I agree and follow him into an office.

The recovery center is nicely decorated with calm paintings and living plants. It doesn't look as if they make loony bins like those in the movies. It's open and airy; there is even a large sunroom that allows the sun to shine in.

Otis welcomes me into his office and points to a chair. "Have a seat," he says as he pulls out a folder. "Penny, right?"

"Yes, it's short for Penelope."

He writes down my name. "This has been quite a day for you, hasn't it?" He leans back in his chair to get comfortable. Something tells me that this is going to be a long conversation.

"It really has. I haven't seen or heard from Mom since I was eight. She just disappeared one day."

My face must express the pain that I've lived with since that day because Otis gives me a sincere, "I'm sorry to hear that."

"So what's wrong with her?"

"Well, *wrong* seems like such a negative term, but your mother has schizophrenia. She was dropped off on our doorstep about twelve years ago, she's our third-longest resident." He sits up straighter now.

"Who dropped her off?"

"Let's see." He opens the folder. "It was a Mister Michael Rushford." He looks at me as if that name should ring a bell.

"I have no idea who that is."

"When he dropped her off, he said he couldn't help her anymore and that she was scaring him with the things she was saying." He continues reading from the folder.

"After some time with Iris, I learned that she believed she had a mission. One that would save you."

I think back to sitting at the table with my mom. She was going on about demons and voices, and saying the only way for me to be okay was for her to leave. "Yeah, she mentioned that."

"I know this is a lot, Ms. Wolfe, and I'm sure it will take some time to process. Are you aware that you are her only known, living family member?"

"What about her dad?"

"Looks like Mr. Wolfe passed away two years ago," he says after looking in the file again. He realizes that Mr. Wolfe is related to me and that, judging by my expression, I had no idea of his passing. "I'm sorry if that is news."

It is news, but not bad news. I couldn't care less if that man was alive or dead. "It's okay; we weren't close."

"Does she ever talk about my dad?" I ask, wondering if that Michael guy is my father.

"She doesn't talk much about people…just you. It can be detrimental to bring up something in the past that may be a trigger. I know you have a lot of questions you'd like to ask her, but I'd recommend keeping things light. We don't want anything to upset her and send her into a distressed mental state."

I make a mental note. Just a couple of hours ago, I was ready to throw fire and tell my mother how much

I despised what happened, but that anger has dissipated and turned into sympathy. I now wish she would have stayed with us. I would have taken care of her and protected her from the toxicity of the world. If I had known she was sick, I would have dedicated my life to her.

"Your mother signed a document stating that she would like to live out her days here at the center. Once she felt her mission was accomplished, she realized that she wasn't well and didn't want to be a burden on anybody. She only had this realization after taking the proper medications, so it's very important that she not miss any doses. That is why I was urgently pushing her to get back here."

He slides the folder towards me. "Now, being that your mother can't care for herself, her assets automatically go to you. She doesn't have much, other than a small lump sum and a house that your grandfather left behind. Everyone makes out a will when they arrive. Unfortunately, your mother didn't have anyone to help her with one, so we supplied an attorney. Your mother had only you, so you are automatically the beneficiary."

My mind is fried at this point. I don't know what any of this means.

I must have a confused look on my face because Otis tries to reassure me by saying, "We have an on-site attorney that handles matters like this. We can set up a meeting with her so she can better explain things to you."

I nod in agreement.

"I don't know if this helps, but I've been taking care of your mom since shortly after she arrived. She has a very caring soul. She might be sick, but she loves you."

"How do you know that?" I ask him almost defensively.

"Come. Let me show you something."

We leave his office and walk towards a big, open room. There are tables with game boards, a big-screen TV, a ping-pong table, and a little library. He walks me into a smaller adjacent room and flicks on the light.

"This is our art room. Your mother spends most of her free time in here." He opens a closet. "This is your mother's closet. She paints more than anyone here, and we didn't want to throw her art away. She's so talented. So we store most of her work in here." He points to a row of shelves and stacked paintings.

Then he picks one up. "You're in almost every painting." He hands it to me.

It's our home in Coupeville; I recognize the backyard. The sky is amber, and our garden is plentiful. I am in the middle of the backyard, wearing a blue dress; my arms are in the air, and I'm in mid-twirl. Butterflies are surrounding me, as if they are dancing with me.

My face turns warm, and I feel as if I am going to cry. "Can I keep this?"

"Absolutely." He smiles.

A woman peeks her head in. "Otis, she's awake," she says and then gives me a smile.

"Shall we?" Otis says.

I follow him to what seems to be my mother's room. It's plastered with her art, and he was right—a little girl ranging from ages one to eight is in almost every single one. She has her own bathroom with a big bathtub and a nice-size closet. Her bed is adorned with a plush ruby comforter and large beige pillow with tassels. A rocking chair sits in the corner, next to a small bookcase full of romance and mystery novels. I notice the sides of the bookshelf are decorated with hand-painted flowers. The entire room looks as if it were plucked from a *Cottage Living* magazine, and it's quite pleasant.

When Mom sees me, her eyes widen, and she smiles. "Penny, you're here!" She opens her arms and gives me a hug.

This hug makes me nearly fall to the ground, but her grip on me steadies my body and keeps me from toppling over. My eyes sting, and I can't help but let them leak. I've longed for this hug for so many years. Her hair smells the same as it always did—a mixture of eucalyptus and strawberry. I'm almost taller than she, but I still feel like a little girl in her arms. I can't hold back the tears, but for the first time in my life, they are happy ones.

CHAPTER TWENTY-ONE

I had a meeting with the recovery center's lawyer a few days ago. Apparently, since my mother has been with them so long, the state has pretty much adopted her, and they pay for her stay since she is mentally unable to take care of herself or be left alone.

When my grandfather died, all of his assets went to my mother; then they were frozen due to my mother's mental state. But they have now been unfrozen and gifted to me. So I am now the owner of Grandpa's house in Port Townsend, along with a small amount of money. I plan to hold on to it in case Mom needs it one day. It doesn't feel like my money, and I wish a piece of Grandpa weren't sitting in my bank account.

I've been visiting my mom every morning before work. I bring her a coffee and some kind of pastry; we spend about an hour or so chatting and having our daily intake of caffeine together.

Some time ago, I also got a full tour of her art closet; she even gave me some to take home. I've put a couple of her paintings up in my apartment. She has such a beautiful technique; her perfectly blended colors make every inch of the canvas pop.

I haven't even seen Ben since last week. I called him and gave him the rundown on what's going on with my mom, without getting into too much detail. He was supportive and told me to let him know if I needed anything. He's been busier than I have, and if I were being honest with myself, I'd say that I have been pretty detached from Ben.

Finding my mother, even with the current circumstances, is something I have needed since forever ago. I needed closure to fill that emptiness in my soul. Now that she's finally in my life again, and that I understand what happened, I feel stronger. I fear that Ben was just something sweet to fill a sour hole.

As I sit on the phone with a realtor, I've decided that I'm going to sell Grandpa's house. I've been told the backyard is a mess, and all of its once-beautiful landscaping is now dead, along with Grandpa, or overgrown. Sadness pokes at me when I think about the garden I had in the backyard and what memories it held. Beautiful, blurred flashbacks of my mom in our flower garden …and, of course, everything Myles.

"People have shown more interest in living in Port Townsend these days. I don't think we will have a problem getting this place sold," the realtor Sherry tells me. "What would you like to do with the belongings inside?"

"We can hire someone to scrap it all. There's nothing of value in there."

"Okay, I am going to get on this, and I'll call you with updates." She says goodbye, and we hang up.

I can't believe what has happened in the last week. Sometimes I have to pinch myself to make sure I'm not dreaming. I am reunited with my mother. If I had known she was sick, my entire life up until now would have been so different. It's funny how these things work out. We never really understand why things happen until later on down the road.

Still, I have so many questions. Why is Mom sick? Why did Grandpa beat me? Why did Grandma not stand up for me? And, finally, why did Myles and I end up apart?

I suppose the answer could be that I needed the heaviness to pull me into a world in which I could thrive. I wasn't going to get here easily; that's for sure.

One thing that has been on my mind is this situation-ship I have with Ben. It was spontaneous, hot, heavy, and exactly what I needed in the moment. But now it is almost a burden. I think Ben may feel the same, considering we don't take much time out of our worlds for each other anymore, which was part of the deal from the beginning. Now that I have more to focus on and live for, I feel I need to rip off the Band-Aid and set us both free.

I take out my phone and send him a text.

Penny: Hey, could we meet up tonight?

Ben: Sure, I'll come by around 8.

I ordered pizza for Ben and me. He arrived just shortly after eight.

"So how is it going at work?" I ask him in between bites.

"It's crazy. I don't know how I'm even alive right now." He scarfs down another piece of pizza as if he hadn't eaten all day.

"Do you have enough brain space for us to talk?" I ask him, wiping my hands on a napkin.

He stops eating and gives me his full attention. "I do," he says with a concerned look.

We sit next to each other on the couch, and I hold his hand. "I think we should stop doing whatever it is we are doing. I really just need a friend right now, more than anything else."

He slowly nods in agreement. "I'm glad you brought this up, actually." He pauses and lets go of my hand. "Sophia called."

Sophia, his long-lost love.

"Wow, what did she have to say?" I ask, oddly excited for him.

"Well, she's still engaged, but she told me she missed me and that she'd like to meet for dinner...just to catch up."

I'm not sure if that's the smartest idea on Ben's part, but I can't express that thought out loud; the smile on his face is too big. "You're okay with that?" I ask instead.

"I know her. I know what this means. She's not happy with him, and she's feeling out if there is anything left between us."

"I'm glad you're happy about this. Just be careful. Your heart is fragile." I smile.

"Are you going to be okay?" He looks for answers in my eyes.

"I'm more than okay right now, Ben." I lay my head on his shoulder and let him caress my arm.

I never thought Ben would be the genuine guy that he has turned out to be. "I'll still be here for you if you need anything. Okay?" he whispers.

I close my eyes and appreciate this moment and all others before it, even the bad ones. If I could lock this feeling in a fireproof box, I would. I have almost found my perfect peace. I am complete, except for one thing—or person, rather.

Ben and I sit together a while longer, drawing out the bittersweet goodbye. We realize it's time for both of us to be on our way, so we untangle, and he makes his way to the front door.

Before he leaves, he turns around and gives me one last kiss. "I hope you find your way back to Myles."

I hope I do too.

CHAPTER TWENTY-TWO

"I can't wait for this party!" Amelia squeals on our lunch break at work. She's excited that I was able to get a spot at the art studio a few weeks from now, but she keeps calling it a party. Which I guess is somewhat true. We will be serving cocktails and appetizers. And Amelia's cousin plays the guitar, so he happily offered to play some acoustic music there.

"I'm excited too," I say, smiling. "I just hope we can get enough people to show up."

"We will. Maybe we should make some flyers or something," she suggests.

"We could, but word of mouth is so much more authentic."

I suddenly get an idea. Alice, the art collector I met in Seattle—maybe I can shoot her an email and tell her about my event. She's *got* to have friends in Southern California who are interested in art.

"I actually might be able to get someone to help on this." I take out my phone and send an email to Alice Dalford.

> *Hi, Alice,*
>
> *My name is Penelope. You bought one of my pieces from the most recent Seattle Art exhibit at the convention center. I will be having my own art event here in Pacific Beach, San Diego, in a few weeks, and I'm looking to get some more foot traffic. Do you have any friends out here that would be interested in attending?*
>
> *I would appreciate any support!*
>
> *Thank you in advance.*
>
> *Sincerely,*
> *Penelope Wolfe*

I add the date, time, and location of the event at the bottom of the email, along with my phone number.

I explain to Amelia how I met Alice. "Let's cross our fingers that she knows someone."

"I'm sure she does. Who flies from New York to Seattle for art? Art geeks, that's who," she says and takes a bite of her sandwich. "My family will be there...and Scott." She blushes a little.

I'm a little surprised to hear that Amelia and Scott are still a thing. "Scott? You must really like him," I tease.

"I really do. He's not like the other guys; he's such a gentleman and seems to really like me."

"Your parents will be there too? Does that mean he's meeting them?"

"Well, Mom and Dad will be there earlier in the evening. Scott is coming by later, but there may be an overlap." She giggles. "I'm not worried about it. My parents will love him."

She's right; her parents are supportive in all ways. They expressed their happiness for me when I told them about my mom. We dove pretty deep into the depths of my childhood; even unbothered Amelia got teary-eyed when I told her how much I had craved seeing my mother again. They even made some homemade zucchini bread for me to take to her. Mom and I shared it while we watched a rom-com in the recreation room.

"Break's over; let's get moving," I say, hopping off the barstool.

CHAPTER TWENTY-THREE

I bought a little black dress to wear to my showcase. I accessorized it with an array of sparkly bracelets and red heels.

Amelia, Scott, and I set up everything last night so we wouldn't have to worry about it much today. I think Amelia was right when she said she felt that Scott really likes her. He was eager to help us when she asked him, and he looked at her all puppy-in-love-eyed the whole time.

I am heading down to the studio early. Otis said he'd bring my mom over to see it before the crowd gets there, assuming there is a crowd.

Mom walked in with a huge smile on her face. "Penny, this is amazing, and you look beautiful," she says, hugging me.

"Thanks, Mom." I smile.

Mom—I've grown comfortable calling her that.

"Look over here. I have something to show you." I guide her to the spot where I have set up her artwork behind red-velvet ropes. Mostly paintings of a younger me in various nature settings. They are so elegant; I can't let them go unseen. "I'm not selling them. I just want people to see where I got my creativity."

She stands there, looking at her artwork. Tears start to form in her eyes. "Honey…thank you," she says, smiling at me. "You are sincerely amazing." She looks at me a little while longer and then turns back towards her art.

I see guilt in her posture. I know somewhere deep inside of her there is some clarity. A true reality that reminds her of her absence and how much she has missed out on being a mother. A reminder that she left her daughter without a parent, and a hint of the pain that is carried with that.

I hope in that same depth she understands that it's not her fault. She was raised in the wrong environment by the wrong people. Her illness needed attention and care, but she received neither.

She stays a little while longer, until Otis reminds her that it's almost time for evening meds and some good-quality sleep. She congratulates me again and makes me promise that I will come see her tomorrow to let her know how it went.

Amelia and her parents arrive shortly after my mom leaves. "This is going to be awesome!" she shrieks. Leslie, Finn, and Kaiden are close behind her.

"Okay, Penny, what can I buy for, like, twenty bucks here?" Kaiden looks around; his parents laugh.

"Hmm, let's see." I walk towards the back and grab a small painting of a palm tree in the moonlight. "How about this?" I suggest.

"That's only twenty dollars?" His smile grows.

"For you, yes," I say and place it in a brown paper bag.

Leslie and Finn mouth, *"thank you,"* knowing that I could have made a pretty penny for that one. People are suckers for palm trees. But I adore Kaiden and wouldn't want it to go to anyone else. So I let him keep the twenty and tell him he just owes me a surfing lesson.

The mobile bartender we hired starts to set up in the back corner, along with the caterer who will be serving shrimp appetizers. Amelia's cousin Zach is here and ready to roll as well.

Before too long, this place is packed. I'm shocked to see so many people. A lot of Alice's friends came and already claimed a few paintings. Even Ben sent me a "good luck" text, along with a bunch of celebratory emojis.

After a few hours of mingling, I'm exhausted. I find a seat in the back and watch the crowd ooh and aah over my artwork. *What a satisfying feeling.* I look at everyone's face and watch their expressions as they move from one piece to the other.

I see Amelia and Scott up close and personal, flirting and sneaking in a kiss here and there. Amelia twirls her hair around a finger, and Scott watches her every move. I think he may adore her just as much as she adores him.

Then I see a very familiar face. A face that holds a soul that I will always cherish. One that makes my stomach weak with unconditional love.

My first thought—*What is he doing here?*

My second thought—*I'm so incredibly happy he is here!*

Myles sees me looking at him, and he smiles. I wonder how long he's been watching me. He starts to walk towards me, so I stand up and meet him halfway. When we are close enough, he immediately pulls me into a hug.

"I'm so proud of you, Penny," he whispers in my ear.

My body softens with the sound of his voice and the embrace of his hug. "Myles, what are you doing here?" The adrenaline running through me isn't helping me wrap my head around the fact that Myles Ford is yet again standing in front of me.

"The truth?" he says, rubbing the back of his head. "I saw your website and noticed you were having an event. I was so impressed that you were doing this; I had to come see it for myself. Plus, it landed during my vacation time, and I've always wanted to visit Southern California." He's still smiling.

He saw it on my website? I don't pay much attention to anyone on social media, and I'm even worse with website inquiries; it's just been a tool for me, and one that seemed to work. I'm glad he saw it, I'm flattered to hear that he keeps up with me, and I'm ecstatic to have him in my presence.

"It's so good to see you." I give him another hug, but this time I linger for a second longer, ignoring the irony of his timing. "Let me show you around."

I walk him around the studio. He seems to enjoy my work, but I catch him looking at me more than at my art.

"How long are you here for?" I ask him as we continue to wander.

"Just a few days. I'm on furlough, so I thought I'd visit and escape the rain a bit." He continues, "I flew in last night. Have you tried that burger joint down the street?" He points in the general direction. "It's so good."

"I have actually; it's one of my favorite spots."

We stop in front of my mom's paintings, and it suddenly hits me that Myles has no idea that I found her.

Despite all the times I wanted to look him up, call him, and tell him, I never did.

I turn to him. "I found her, Myles."

He looks puzzled for only a moment; then his eyes go wide, and he scoops me into his arms again. When he finally pulls away, he asks, "Is she okay?" He realizes that finding her may not be a positive thing.

"She's okay. It's a long story. She lives in a mental hospital."

He gives me a relieved look. He is the only person who knows how much I needed the truth.

"I'm staying at a hotel down the street, and I'd really like it if we could catch up. I know you're busy tonight with all of this, bu—"

I interrupt him, "Actually, I'm starving. Let's go get one of those burgers."

He grins and nods. "After you."

"Let's sneak out the back," I suggest and grab my purse on the way out.

It only took about ten minutes to walk to the burger place, but by the time we got there, it seemed as if no time had passed since Myles and I were last together.

Just like in the hotel room in Seattle.

Our relationship is timeless, and that is something for which I'm so grateful.

"So that's when I saw her for the first time since I was eight. It was just fate, I guess." I tell Myles how this new relationship with my mother has unfolded.

We each ordered burgers, fries, and a milkshake to share.

"Penny, I don't even know what to say. I'm so happy for you," he tells me with half a French fry in his mouth. It's amazing the attention and conversation he can hold while eating a meal.

"Enough about me. Are you in a firemen's calendar yet?" I joke.

"Ha, not yet, but I was just promoted to lieutenant. That's why I'm taking furlough right now. I needed a break before the heavy workload I am about to have."

"I'm glad to see that you're living out your childhood dreams. Do you remember how badly you wanted to be a firefighter?" I giggle.

"Yes, I'm almost embarrassed at how obsessed I was." He laughs with me.

A second of awkward silence grows, which is foreign to us.

"I'm just going to address the elephant in the room," he blurts. "I know we said our goodbyes in Seattle, but I haven't felt content about that. We were so close, and nothing has felt normal since that day I left." He looks humble as he pauses in between sentences.

"When I saw that you were going to exhibit at an art gallery, something inside told me that I needed to be here." He takes a much-needed sip of water. "I guess I just miss you, Penny." He looks at me with sincerity in his eyes.

"I haven't felt the same either, Myles. There were so many times I wanted to reach out," I say, feeling sorry that I didn't. "I'm really glad you came. Your timing is perfect." I give him a genuine smile.

He reaches across the table and places my hands inside of his. We stare at each other for a minute, or maybe it was longer than that; time seems to diminish when I'm with him. In the eyes of this man, I see the boy who saved my life by just simply being himself.

We are interrupted by the waitress with our check. "Thank you," I tell her and try to take the check.

"No, no, I got this," Myles says, putting his card with the bill.

"Okay, I'll get it next time. Thanks."

He shakes his head as if that's never going to happen. Myles has always been the old-school gentleman. I remember, even as teenagers, he'd open the car door for me, pay for my meals, and walk on the side closest to the street on sidewalks.

"So, um, when *is* the next time? I'm sure you're busy, and you know I have commitments with the beach and all" — he awkwardly laughs — "but, if we could hang out again before I leave, that would be really cool." I almost see desperation in his eyes, as if he needs this encounter just as much as I do.

"We are spending every second we have together," I reassure him. "Would you like to see my mom?" I ask him, hoping that's not totally inappropriate.

"More than anything." He smiles.

"Where are you staying again?"

"At the Courtyard, just down the street."

"Okay, I'll pick you up tomorrow morning. She's usually up early, and I try to see her before work."

"Sounds great." He finishes paying the bill and walks me back to the art gallery.

"I know I keep saying this, but I'm truly happy that you are here."

"I am too," he says, pulling me in and resting his chin on top of my head.

"I'll see you bright and early."

I watch him walk down the street. He walks tall; his broad shoulders give his silhouette such a manly look, and before I look away, he looks back at me and smiles...*the best smile.*

CHAPTER TWENTY-FOUR

I pull up to the Courtyard Hotel and see Myles waiting on a bench out front.

"Oh my God," he says, referring to my Bronco, "you still have this thing?"

"It's with me until one of us dies."

We laugh. His laugh warms my body; I've missed it. In the corners of his eyes, he's developed small wrinkles that are exaggerated when he smiles. When I lived in Port Townsend, I felt that he looked like a man, but he screams testosterone even more so now. Maybe it's because he's a lieutenant in the fire department; that has got to have given him extra man points.

On our way to the recovery center, I point out some good food spots he should try and some secret entryways to the beach. We pass by the parking lots in which I used to park my Bronco and sleep. I tell Myles all of my tales about being homeless.

"You've really come a long way." He smiles at me. "You're kind of incredible, Penny."

I blush. The last time I saw Myles, he kissed me. Now he's sitting in my car with me, over a thousand miles away from his home.

Last night I could barely sleep, thinking about why he's here. I mean, obviously, he chose this destination because I am here; he flat out told me that.

I wonder if he came here to try to talk me into going back home with him. Maybe this time apart has been too long, and he's just done living without me. That would be a beautiful love story if it were true.

Even if it were, though, I can't leave—my mom is here, and she needs me. He can't leave his home either; his whole life is in Seattle.

We get to the center and check in. Myles looks around, admiring the décor.

"It's pretty nice, right?" I ask him as we wait.

"It's not bad at all. In fact, it's pretty damn fancy."

I admire his ease with everything he says; he's always been such a calming presence.

One of the staff members greets us and walks us to my mom. She's in the recreational room, reading a book. She sees us almost immediately and jumps up with a huge smile. "How did it go?" She greets me with hug.

"It went really well." I hug her back.

She turns and looks at Myles. "I'm assuming you are my Penelope's boyfriend of some sort?" she asks him, holding out her hand for a handshake.

He chuckles a little. "I'm a longtime friend," he tells her and shakes her hand.

She smiles. "Come sit with me," she says and waves us over to a nearby couch.

My mother is immediately interested in knowing Myles. She asks where he came from and thinks she may even recognize him. When he tells her that he used to be our neighbor, it clicks. "Oh yes, the little boy that always had a fire truck in his hand, right?"

She remembers, and he blushes. I don't recall Myles much before fifth grade, but apparently Mom does.

"All that practice playing with fire trucks paid off; I'm a lieutenant now."

"The girls must love that," Mom says and winks at me. "So if you're not with Penny, do you have a lover back home?"

This question bothers me. It's crossed my mind that Myles could have a girlfriend. Why wouldn't he? He's the full package and then some.

"I don't," he says and looks at me out of the corner of his eye.

"That's too bad. You seem like such a nice guy." She pretends to squeeze his biceps, which makes us all laugh.

I love watching Myles and my mom talk. They feed off each other's energy and seem to enjoy each other's company. Myles is a natural with her, just as he always was with me. Soothing wounded women must be his specialty.

We stay long enough to sit and have breakfast with Mom. The recovery center has a surprisingly good selection of pancakes, waffles, and muffins.

Unfortunately, I have to work, so we say our goodbyes. "I'll come back soon, Mom."

"You better." She gives Myles and me both a kiss on the cheek.

"She's pretty great, Penny. You guys are almost identical," Myles says once we are back in the car.

"Yeah, that's the one thing I remember most about her. It took me a little bit to accept everything; you know more than anybody how her absence affected me. I'm just grateful that I have her now."

"I'm really glad that you do too." He smiles at me.

"I have to get to work, but I'm going to let them know I won't be in for a couple of days so I can show you around," I say while starting up the Bronco.

He smiles at me. "I'm free tonight, tomorrow, and literally this entire trip. It was planned on a whim." He takes out his phone. "I should probably have your number."

I don't know why Myles's asking for my number gives me butterflies, but I feel as if I were a schoolgirl finally getting asked to prom by her crush.

I drop him off back at his hotel, wishing I didn't have to go to work. I'd much rather stay here with Myles.

"I'll see you soon," he says and hops out.

We have such limited time together that having to go serve food to random people seems as if it's such a trivial thing to do.

Chapter Twenty-Five

Halfway through my shift, I get a text.

> *Myles: So would you mind showing me around Pacific Beach tomorrow?*

His request makes me smile. There's nothing more I'd rather do.

> *Penny: Yes! I'll call you after work.*

I immediately go to the manager's office and pop my head in. I'm pretty sure Mike smokes weed for breakfast, lunch, and dinner, yet he has somehow become the boss of this place.

"Hey, Mike, do you mind if I take a few days off?"

"Go for it; just write it down on the whiteboard."

All the staff write down their schedules on a white-board, and by the looks of it, they won't really need me this week. *Ironic how the universe works.*

Amelia comes up behind me. "Where ya going?"

"Nowhere. I have an old friend visiting," I tell her, capping the marker.

"The friend you snuck off with the other night?" She winks.

"Actually, yes." I blush.

"He's a hottie. You gonna hit that or what?" She pretends to make out with her hand.

"He's my friend." I roll my eyes even though, in the back of my mind, I wouldn't mind doing exactly that.

Nearly every shift at Coral's Café has been busy since I started working here. Every single one...until today. I think some higher being is playing a trick on me. Gifting me boredom so my mind runs wild with intrusive thoughts and counts the seconds until I get to leave and go see Myles.

Eventually, my shift ends. I call Myles.

"Hey," he answers.

"Hey, did you get to explore at all today?"

"Kind of. I had some good tacos, but I mostly hung out at the pool. Something I don't get to do in Seattle."

"The weather is the best."

"It really is. What are you up to?"

"I'm coming over; let's go night swimming."

"Yeah? Okay, I'll meet you in the lobby," he says, sounding excited, and hangs up.

All of this feels so weird—having him here and spending this time with him. It almost feels as if we were in a whole different world and in another lifetime.

When I arrive, Myles is sitting in the lobby, waiting for me. He's shirtless in swim trunks and sandals. *Wow.* The firefighter career has done him well.

He looks up and sees me. We greet each other, his partially crooked smile makes me swoon.

"Right this way," he says and leads me to the pool area. "They close at ten, but I feel like people out here don't really care about that. I heard some people at midnight last night."

I dip my toes in the pool; it's heated and a perfect temperature. Before I can look back at Myles, a giant splash soaks me.

He reemerges from underwater and says, "Did I forget to say cannonball?" and laughs.

I shake my head, smiling, and slip off my shorts and T-shirt. I typically wear swimsuits under my clothes because a quick beach session isn't ever out of the norm. I jump in next to him, trying to make my own big splash.

"Not bad, Wolfe, not bad," he mocks me.

We take turns doing laps in the pool, timing each other to see how long it takes, as if we were little kids competing to see who can hold their breath longer. Finally, I sit on the steps in the shallow end of the pool.

Myles wades in front of me. "It's nice out here" —he looks around and admires the sky—"but nothing beats the PNW," he says, looking at me now.

"I know what you mean. I like San Diego, but my heart belongs to Washington."

He gets closer to me. "Just Washington?"

My arms start to tingle. I can almost feel his breath on my face. "I miss a lot of things about it," I say, trying not to sound rattled.

"Washington misses you too," he says, so close that his lips can almost touch mine.

Suddenly, the gate slams shut, and an older couple walks in and sets up near the Jacuzzi. The loud bang of the gate startles both Myles and me, and he moves to sit next to me.

What timing.

"I appreciate you taking some time to show me around out here. I know this was unexpected, but I want to get the most out of this trip," Myles says before adding, "which involves you."

I smile. "I've been thinking about you since I ran into my mom."

"Oh yeah?" He smirks.

"You were there for me the entire time. Being around her takes me back to those dark places sometimes. The times when I needed her, like when I was scared or sad, or if I just needed a hug. It was always you who showed up." I look at him sincerely. "I owe you."

He shakes his head. "You don't owe me, Penny. You gave to me just as much as I gave to you."

"How is that?"

"You were my best friend; almost all of my childhood stories have you in them."

"I'm sorry I left."

"You did the right thing; I didn't want you in that house one minute longer than you had to be. I'm sorry that I even expected that."

We sit in silence for a few more minutes. "I should probably get going; it's kind of late," I say, stepping out of the pool.

Myles nods and stands up too, but before he follows me, out of the corner of my eye, I see him scan my body. His glance reminds me of the time by the lake on our field trip to the marina. He follows me out of the pool and grabs us both towels from the storage shelf.

"Thanks."

"So what's the plan tomorrow?" he asks while drying off.

"Well, we are in San Diego, and the beaches are pretty nice. So I think we should have a full-on beach day."

He smiles. "That sounds amazing."

"I can pick you up whenever."

"How about I pick you up instead? I have a rental car."

"Okay, that works. I'll text you my address." I slip my clothes on over the swimsuit.

Myles walks me to my car. The sky is clear, and the air is warm. *If he asks me if I want to go upstairs with him, I won't say no.* It almost seems silly that we aren't planning to spend every waking and sleeping moment together. Testing the waters, and trying to figure out what is appropriate and what isn't, is hard when you're with the guy with whom you have always been infatuated.

I try to remind myself that this visit will come to an end, and spending the night with Myles will just make it harder than it already will be to say goodbye.

"Thanks for coming by," Myles says once we reach my car. He opens the door for me, but stands in the way. He lightly grasps my hips and pulls me into him.

Is he going to kiss me?

He looks at my face and leans in. I close my eyes and start to pucker my lips, but I feel a gentle kiss on my cheek, rather than on my perked lips. I open my eyes to see him pulling away.

"Goodnight, Penny," he says, smiling, and walks back towards the hotel.

I should be embarrassed, but instead I immediately replay the feeling that kiss just gave me. I take a deep breath, get in my car, and drive home.

Chapter Twenty-Six

Myles drives up to my place in a bright-red sports car; he's wearing a black tank top and Ray-Bans.

I decided on a pink bikini with jean shorts, which seems to have been a good idea—I notice Myles admiring my decision. I see his jaw tense up a little bit when I get in the car. I think my entire body tensed up a little too. He's gotten a tan the last couple of days that he's been here, and the way the sun is hitting his biceps has me a little flustered.

"Nice ride," I say.

"You like it? It's pretty obnoxious." He laughs.

"Okay, so obviously this whole town is basically a beach, but there is a little spot in more of a residential area that doesn't have hundreds of tourists. Plus, there's a pretty good food shack nearby."

"Just tell me the way." He smiles.

We listen to music and talk as if we were in high school all over again. As though no time has passed between us. The same comfort level is present, just as it was years ago. Except for one big difference—I am more attracted to Myles than I have ever been before.

A text from Amelia disrupts my lustful thoughts.

> *Amelia: Hey, girl. I hope you are having fun with your "friend." I need to meet him.*
>
> *Penny: LOL. Okay. I'll try to figure something out.*

"Is that your…uh…boyfriend?"

"No. It's my friend Amelia. She wants to meet you."

He stays quiet for a minute, looking as if he's trying to muster up the courage to ask an uncomfortable question. It's a little weird seeing him uncomfortable; Myles was always the confident one.

"Do you have a boyfriend?" he finally asks.

There it is, and I'm glad he finally asked because I've been quite curious about his love life too.

"No."

He adjusts himself in his seat. "Me either. Not even a recent breakup. My schedule complicates relationships.

I dated this girl for a while. She was cool, but for some reason, I couldn't embrace the relationship."

"I understand that completely," I say, thinking of Ben.

We pull up to the residential neighborhood and find a parking spot in front of a big white house. We grab our things and set up under a palm tree on the beach.

"This is awesome," he says while laying out his towel.

"Yeah, I do this at least once a week," I say, sitting next to him on the sand.

Myles starts to laugh a little under his breath.

"What's so funny?"

"I just can't believe I'm sitting here with you. When I found out that you left that day, I didn't think I'd ever see you again." He pauses and looks at me. "And now I've seen you twice in the same year."

I look at him and offer a small smile. "It's pretty great, huh?"

"Yes, it is. I just wonder what comes after."

"After?" I ask, hoping this conversation will go the way we both want it to.

"Well, trying to pursue a friendship or...uh... any type of relationship would be impossible in our situation. You finally have your mom and a solid life," he says, looking away.

"What do you mean by any other type of relationship?" I ask him, stuck on that part of his sentence.

"Penny, really?" His eyes are focused on me now; his smile is gone, but his body language is still calm. "I kissed you that night."

I smile, remembering that kiss.

He catches me smiling. He's probably remembering it the same way I am because he starts to smile too.

I wish I could allow my heart to indulge completely in this time with Myles, but he's leaving, and I don't know if I can handle that heartbreak.

"Are you hungry?" I ask, changing the subject.

"I could eat."

"Let me go grab some food for us."

He raises his hand. "Let me get it," he says, standing up. "I'll be right back."

I watch as he walks towards the food stand. The dimples on his lower back glisten with sweat, and his legs are muscular and manly. My heart folds with the thought of loving him. Love...lust. Two very different things. Two things I feel completely with Myles.

I shake my head and turn back toward the ocean. *I'm not helping myself here.*

Myles returns with the food, and we eat in peaceful silence. There are only a few other people on the beach. A man with his dog, and a mother and child.

I never thought much of having kids. I think the abandonment by my mother and the abuse by my grandfather steered me away from the idea of having children. I know I am much different than both of them, but even the slightest idea that I could cause so much pain to any person who relies on me makes me sick to my stomach.

Myles finishes his food and stares into the water; he closes his eyes and breathes in the salty air. I like seeing him relaxed. I almost want to reach out and comb my fingers through his hair to make sure he is real.

"Shall we test the water?" he asks, opening his eyes a few moments later.

"Absolutely."

We get up and walk side by side into the water. It's chilly but refreshing. Myles dives in, completely getting lost in a wave. "Come on!" he yells, resurfacing a few yards away.

I jump in after him. We barge the waves and splash around like little kids. It's the most fun I've had in a long time.

Eventually the waves, salt, and sun tire us out. So we make our way back to our towels. "That was fun," he says, out of breath. "I've never played in the ocean like that before."

"You know, I haven't either. Amelia and I usually just sun tan and dip our toes in here and there."

"I'm glad you have her. Sounds like you two get along," he says, wiggling his toes in the sand.

"She's great."

The sun is starting to set, and the temperature starts to drop a bit. "Do you want to head back to my place? We can order dinner, or I can make some pasta or something."

He doesn't hesitate. "I'd love to."

"Nice place," Myles comments.

"I don't need much."

I haven't added furniture since moving in. I have the necessities, with the exception of a few decorative pieces. I've learned to enjoy the simpler things. Clutter reminds me of the house back in Port Townsend, which still hasn't sold.

"I'll give you the grand tour," I say, setting my things down on the counter. I walk Myles through the living room to the balcony.

"I knew some kind of plant life would be out here." He chuckles.

"Yeah, this is my mini Zen garden." I giggle because of the lack of space or even an actual garden.

I show him my room next; two of my mom's paintings are hung above my bed. My comforter matches the pillow's deep-forest-green color.

"Do you live alone in Seattle?"

"Yeah, I do. I used to have a roommate; one of the fire captains stayed with me for a while, but he was transferred," he says, plopping down on the couch.

I join him. "Is being a fireman everything you had hoped for?"

"It is. Not only is the job itself rewarding, but everyone at the firehouse treats each other as family. It's very close-knit, a good support system."

I like the idea of that kind of support. It makes me think of my life here with Amelia and her family, and now my own mom. I can't help but let sadness infiltrate my thoughts, thinking of how lonely I used to be. *Sometimes those old feelings haunt me.*

"What's wrong?" Myles asks, noticing my change in demeanor.

"Oh nothing. You hungry?" I ask, trying to change the subject.

"You must have forgotten who I am," he says, turning his body towards me. Myles could always tell when something was off.

I lean back into the couch. "It just gets lonely here, I guess. I'm always so submerged in my art and work that I don't think about it much. I have Amelia, and now my mom in some ways, but..." I stop to collect my thoughts.

"No one understands you."

No one understands me.

"Exactly," I whisper.

Myles scoots a little closer to me and holds my hand. "I understand you," he whispers back.

I direct my face to his and look into his eyes; he says his words so sincerely. He is the only person on this planet who fully understands me. If I were to ask him to drop his life in Washington, I think he'd do it.

The moment is so pure and full of love that I can't help but demand, "Kiss me," in a whisper.

There is no hesitation on his end; his face moves slowly to mine until our lips touch. His tongue slowly pushes through into my mouth. It's soft and warm, and the movements of our tongues are in harmony.

He gently pulls me closer to his body; he smells salty—a mixture of ocean air and sweat. His hand moves up my back and onto the back of my head. My heart begins to race heavily as his other hand runs down my thigh.

Our kiss is strong, and there is no going back. Both of his hands are on my thighs now; his fingers tense and dig slightly into my skin. I let out a light moan.

He pulls me onto him. Straddling him, I push my body harder into his; his arms are holding me now. I pull back and untie my bikini top; his eyes don't leave my face until I drop my top to the floor. Then they move to my breasts. His face follows, and he slowly kisses each one of them.

I stand up and slip off my shorts...and then my bikini bottoms. I stay there and let him study me for a minute before I turn and walk into my bedroom. I feel his eyes watch my every move before he gets up to follow me.

I lie down on my bed and watch as Myles undresses. His body is beautiful and masculine; I want every part of him. He lies next to me and pulls me on top of him.

His next kiss is fierce and more passionate than before. He's hard, and I can't help but touch him.

He shivers and whispers, "Oh my God."

I like that I am pleasing him, so I rub him a little more.

His head rolls back into the pillow, and he closes his eyes. Only moments pass before he pulls me close so he can kiss me again.

"Penny, I want you so bad," he whispers in my ear.

I don't hesitate to adjust myself and lower my body onto his. He's inside of me, and I moan.

He rolls me over so he's on top of me now and gently thrusts into me.

He makes love to me.

Words can't explain how incredible this felt. Our first time was precious, as if it were a gem you'd keep safe inside a locked box. This time, I felt my soul fall deeper into a love that I didn't know existed. His body merged with mine; that's where it was meant to be. We fit together like puzzle pieces.

He pulls out and finishes in the T-shirt that he'd thrown down at the end of the bed. He comes back to me and pants heavily while lying next to me. He takes me into his arms and guides my head to his chest.

I listen to his heartbeat and wonder if there was ever a sound more comforting than this. *I've never felt so at home.*

"Do you remember the last time we did this?" he asks, breaking the silence.

"Of course I do. It was the night you told me that you loved me," I say sleepily.

"I did say that, didn't I?" He lets out a light laugh.

"You sure did."

"That was the best night of my life," he says confidently.

"Will you stay here with me tonight?" I ask, hoping that we can make this temporary bliss an all-nighter.

"Of course, I will," he says and starts to rub my head.

I drift into a foreign slumber. Safe, comfortable, full of love, full of desire. I listen to Myles's heartbeat, loving the fact that his heart is so close to mine; our skin touching is all the warmth I need. I even dream of a distant whisper—*I love you.*

Chapter Twenty-Seven

I wake up to the smell of breakfast. *Am I still dreaming?* The aroma of pancakes and bacon fill the apartment. I look around to see that Myles has gotten up, and I hear him quietly opening and closing cupboards.

I slip out of bed and into a silky robe. "Smells amazing," I say as I enter the kitchen.

"I hope so; this is about all I know how to make." He puts down the spatula and walks around the counter until he meets me. He pulls me into his shirtless body and gives me a kiss on top of my head.

My body melts into his, and for the moment, nothing is wrong with the world.

"It'll be ready in about twenty minutes," he says, going back to work.

"I'll go shower quickly," I say and head to the bathroom.

I take a quick shower; it's a little bit melancholy. I almost feel guilty about washing his scent off me. If I weren't on the pill, I'd be a little worried about pregnancy. Something tells me that, on the odd chance I did wind up pregnant, Myles would be the perfect partner and an even more wonderful father.

I finish my shower, throw on a sundress, and meet Myles back in the kitchen. The table is set, and there are a few wildflowers in a small glass sitting in the middle of the table.

He looks up from dishing pancakes, and he immediately grins. "A dress, huh?"

That night in his truck I wore a sundress, and he best believe this outfit choice was intentional.

He pulls a chair out for me to sit down.

"What a gentleman," I comment. "Where did you find the flowers?"

"Out front. Some older lady looked at me like I was vandalizing property, so I just grabbed a few and ran back in." He chuckles.

"This is really yummy; thank you for doing this," I say, taking bites of the delicious pancake.

"Well, I leave tomorrow. I thought we could make today special," he says solemnly.

I hadn't thought about reality since Myles and I started kissing last night. I've been living a dream for the last twelve hours. Now, here we are, back to the real world. My heart breaks silently, and I can feel the same in Myles.

"Let's just make the best of it," he says to me, forcing a smile onto his face.

I offer a smile back, and we finish our breakfast.

"I thought we could go see your mom this morning, and then maybe act like tourists."

"Like, pretend we are tourists?" I ask to clarify.

"Yeah. Well, I kind of am a tourist." He laughs a little.

"Okay, sounds interesting," I agree and grab my purse.

We run by his hotel so he can put on a shirt and some clean shorts. Then we make our way over to the recovery center.

My mom is in her room, watching TV in bed. She brightens up as soon as we walk in. "Hey, kids," she says, hugging us both.

"Are you feeling okay?" I ask her, sitting in a chair that is positioned diagonally from her bed.

"I'm just very tired today, but so happy to see you both. Did you decide to stay here, Myles?" she asks hopefully.

"I head home tomorrow, unfortunately," he admits.

Sadness fills the air, and I hope that we don't keep bringing that up in every other conversation.

"That's too bad," she says while lying back down.

We stay for a little while longer and then let her get some rest. Otis previously mentioned that my mother has been extra tired the last few days, but he assured me that it's a common side effect of the medication she takes.

"Okay," Myles says once we get back in the car, taking out his phone, "next stop, Fashion Valley." He types it into his GPS.

"Fashion Valley? Do you have an itinerary?" I ask amusedly.

"I sure do." He smiles and revs the engine.

Fashion Valley is a nearby mall, one I have never visited. I haven't splurged on clothing or shoes or really anything that you could get from a mall.

As we drive up to the outdoor shopping center, I'm overwhelmed by the number of stores. I don't even know where to start, and I don't think Myles is the type to know what's "in" right now. But I'm excited to see what this adventure entails.

"I'm spoiling you today," he says as we get out of the car. "We are going to get some new shoes, some fancy art supplies, and whatever else you want."

"Oh, Myles, we don't have to do that. I have everything I need," I say, joining him outside of the car.

"I know, Penny. You are extremely self-sufficient and independent. More than anyone else I know. But have you ever been spoiled like this?" he asks, taking my hands into his.

"Well, no, bu—" I start to answer.

He interrupts me, "No buts. Let's go blow some dough." He holds my hand as we walk in.

Our first stop is a shoe store full of every kind of shoe you can imagine. I spot a pair of fire-truck-red Chucks—my favorite shoe.

Myles notices me admiring them and asks for my shoe size. Before I can protest, he has a box in his hand at the cash register.

"Let's see; we need some new sunglasses." He looks around to find a Sunglass House.

I try on countless pairs until I find the perfect ones. Myles gets a pair too and makes sure to snap a picture of us in our new shades.

When I say this man spoiled me, I mean he SPOILED me. Not only did he treat me to my favorite shoes and a sparkly pair of sunglasses, but our arms were full of canvases and new acrylic paints by the end of the shopping trip. I was tuckered out by the time we were done. Shopping should be its own sport.

"There's one more stop I want to make before we go have lunch at your restaurant."

"We are going to Coral's?"

"Yes, ma'am."

We stand in front of a jewelry store. I admire how everything shines in perfectly lit cases. I don't know if I've been inside a store like this before, unless you count Finn's garage full of lost jewelry.

"Myles, this is more than enough," I say, pointing to everything we are carrying.

"I really want to do this for you, Penny. When was the last time anyone got you jewelry?"

I pause for a second; I feel that he may already know the answer to that question. "I was gifted a necklace for my eighteenth birthday," I finally say.

His face falls from happy to somber. "Oh." He pauses for a second before another smile grows on his face. "I guess that makes me a lucky guy." He leans in and plants a light kiss on my lips. "Come on." He nods toward the store.

The lady working in the front welcomes us. "What are we shopping for today?" she asks energetically.

"Hmm, how about a bracelet?" Myles suggests.

"Okay." I smile.

I decide to embrace the moment and Myles's generosity, so we parade around the store, looking at every option. The lady is more than patient with me when I can't make up my mind.

"I love all of them," I say.

"How much for all?" Myles jokes.

I can't believe how much I adore him.

CHAPTER TWENTY-EIGHT

We picked out a sterling silver bracelet with delicately thin leaves around its circumference. I dangled it around my wrist in the sunlight as we drove to Coral's Café. I thank Myles over and over, to the point that he told me not to thank him anymore—jokingly of course. He said he got enjoyment from watching my excitement, and I believed him.

I knew Amelia was working today, which is good timing because she wants to meet Myles, and he expressed that he would like to meet her too. We sat at an outdoor table, and the host took our drink orders.

"Penny!" I hear Amelia squeal as she walks towards us with a notepad in hand.

I stand up and give her a hug. "This is Myles." I gesture to him.

He stands up and offers his hand.

"It's nice to meet you, Myles," she says while shaking it.

"Nice to meet you too. I've heard a lot of good things about you," he responds and sits down.

Amelia peeks over at me and winks. "So what can I get for you guys?"

"Penny, what's the best here?" he asks, directing his attention towards me.

"The California sub is amazing," I say, ignoring the menu.

"Okay, two of those," he says, closing the menu and handing it to Amelia.

"I'll go put the order in and come back so we can chit-chat a little bit." She smiles.

"She seems sweet," he says, looking around the restaurant and admiring the beachy décor. "It's nice in here."

"It is. I've been working here for a while now," I say, "but my art has been selling pretty consistently. So I might be able to quit and just focus on that soon."

"Your dreams are all coming true." He smiles and takes a drink of his iced tea.

"Most of them."

I know he knows what I mean by that comment. I have fulfilled the dream of finding my mother, and I'm so close to starting my career as an artist, but there's one thing that would ultimately complete me. And that is a life with Myles.

It pains me to know that he will be so far away and that visits like this may never happen again. And even if they do, they will eventually fade away as he and I become busier in life. I can't leave my mom, and I can't take her with me.

Amelia pops back over and interrupts my pessimistic thoughts. She sits next to me and asks, "So, Myles, what do you do for a living?"

"I'm a fire lieutenant back in Washington."

"Wow, sounds like a dangerous job. How did you and Penny meet?"

"At school. I stopped her from beating up Piper Evans in fifth grade." He chuckles.

"Um, I don't know if I've heard this story." She nudges me in the shoulder. "Penny is so sweet and innocent. I can't even imagine her killing a fly."

I roll my eyes because she's half right.

Myles proceeds to tell her about that day and how we were inseparable after it. He left out the details about my grandfather and how I disappeared two months before my eighteenth birthday.

He was right last night; he does understand me. *My secrets are his secrets.*

After what feels like an interrogation, Amelia leaves to go get our food. I'm glad we chose the sandwiches; they are one of my favorite things on the menu, and Myles loves it. Although, we are so hungry from shopping all day that anything would have tasted good.

We finish our food; of course, Myles tries to pay the bill, but I play my "I work here" card and get it comped. Since it was free, he didn't argue.

We say goodbye to Amelia, and she makes me promise to call her when I'm free.

"I have one more thing planned for us tonight," Myles says. "Don't worry; it requires very little energy."

He drives us back to the beach we went to yesterday. He lays out the towels that we had left in the car and pats one, gesturing for me to sit with him. The sun is setting, and the air is cool. He offers me one of a couple of sweatshirts he brought.

I pull it over my head and take a second to breathe in deeply. It smells like Myles, which is so comforting to me.

"Today was amazing, Myles. Thank you so much for everything."

"I had fun today too." He puts his arm around me and pulls me in closer. "I wish our time didn't have to end," he says, squeezing me a little tighter.

"Me too."

"I've been racking my brain, trying to figure out how to make sense of all of this. I came here on a whim, not knowing how you were going to react. My plan was just to congratulate you and tell you how proud I was of you" —he pauses—"but when I saw you, all of that changed."

He adjusts himself to sit deeper in the sand. "I didn't feel like I got the closure I needed in Seattle. When I left, I felt more confused than when I got there. Being with you makes me happy, and when you're gone, I'm lost."

He takes his arm from around me and places his face in his palms. "I feel stupid. How am I supposed to leave tomorrow and not want to turn back? I made that mistake years ago when I left you in Port Townsend. Every piece of me wanted to turn around that day."

I put my arm on his back and start to rub. "Things happened the way they were supposed to. That day was one of the most painful days I've experienced. But, now that I'm here, I know why. I wouldn't have found my mom if you hadn't left, Myles...because I wouldn't have left."

He looks at me and smiles. "You're right, but what does it mean now?" He looks away again.

"I'm not sure. I don't think we will know that until further down the road. Things happen for a reason; sometimes we aren't lucky enough to know why in the moment." My words make me feel a little better, and I think they help Myles too.

"I don't think I can do this again, Penny," he admits, turning his body towards me.

"What do you mean?" I ask, a little shocked by his comment.

"Once I leave, this has to end. The goodbyes are too painful." I see tears start to form in his eyes. "If we somehow end up together again, I won't let you go. Do you hear me, Penny? The next time we are together, I'm not leaving, and I'm not letting you go." He pauses and pulls me into his lap. "I've loved you since I was eleven years old, Penelope," he whispers and kisses me as if he's never kissed me before.

CHAPTER TWENTY-NINE

Myles lies next to me, sleeping peacefully. We made love again last night, and then we showered, had a midnight snack, and cried together. But I still feel that I didn't get enough of him. He leaves this morning and needs to pack up his hotel room before heading to the airport. I've been awake for hours, trying to absorb every moment that he lies here with me. I know his alarm will be sounding any moment now.

I've played the scenario over and over again in my mind—I leave with him, but the angst I feel over leaving my mom hurts too much. It's a double-edged sword. One route leads to being with the one and only man I have ever loved, but takes me away from the woman I've needed all of my life. The other route keeps me with my mother, but tears me away from Myles.

"Is it morning already?" Myles says sadly and opens his eyes.

"Yes," I murmur. Unfortunately, it is morning, and it's time for him to go. I cuddle up close and let him hold me; his chin rests on my head, and I listen to his heartbeat once more.

"I don't want to leave," he admits.

I squeeze his body, reassuring him that the feeling is mutual. Then I gently leave his grasp, get out of bed, and put on a T-shirt and shorts. I watch as he gets dressed, a scene that will never grow old, one that will forever live in my mind.

He gathers his items and stops at the front door. "This is hard," he says.

I feel my eyes start to burn from my trying to hold back the tears. "Very hard," I say and pull him into a hug.

"Maybe in another lifetime," he says, trying to smile. "Goodbye, Penny, I'll always love you."

"I'll always love you too, Myles."

He kisses me one last time and walks out the door.

The second it is completely shut, I fall to the ground and let the tears fall. We had agreed that we would only talk again if we were ready to be together. We are trying to accept that we are the right people, but it is the wrong time.

The pain I feel is so familiar. I felt it when my mom left; I felt it when Myles left—both times. I thought

I knew heartbreak before, but this takes the cake. The last thing I want right now is to be alone, so I race to my car and drive to the recovery center.

"Hi, Mom," I greet her in the recreation room.

"Hi, sweetie." She pauses. "What's wrong?" Even though my mother is still nearly a stranger, she can feel that something is off.

I break down and start crying again.

She rolls me into a hug. "He left?" she asks, even though she already knew the answer.

I let myself cry into her, something I have craved to do since I was eight years old.

She holds me tight and whispers, "It's going to be okay."

I pull myself together and look up at her. "There are some things I need to talk about and get off my chest," I admit.

"I know." She nods in agreement. "Let's go to my room." She walks slowly, still not fully energized after the medication's side effects. When we get to her room, she gestures for me to sit on the bed with her.

"Did Grandpa ever beat you?" I immediately ask.

Her shoulders drop. "Yes," she says quietly.

"Did you think that he was better than whatever demons were after me?"

"I did. He was older, and I thought maybe he had calmed down...he wasn't showing signs of anger when I was there with you."

I nod slowly, trying to find a place of understanding. I remember that I need to tread carefully. "My life up until recently has been really difficult, Mom. I've tried to make sense of it for so long, and just this last year I finally found some clarity. I just wish it hadn't been that way," I say sadly.

She starts to sob. "I'm so sorry, honey." Her breathing becomes irregular, and I realize that this conversation is too much for her.

I rest my hand on her shoulder. "I'm just glad we are together now," I say, rubbing lightly.

The questions I have for her will have to disappear at some point in my life; she's not in any state to confront the past. I don't think she will ever be in a strong enough mindset to give that to me. I don't know if that's because of her guilt or her mental illness. I suppose it really doesn't matter.

Forgiveness has come easy for me; forgetting has not. I don't place the blame on her anymore though; there is no one to blame. This is just the life I was supposed to live. I have so much inner work to do to become trusting and open-minded when it comes to people. I hope that someday I get to that point so I can move on with my life.

But moving on from Myles seems impossible at this point. I've gotten a taste of him that I will never be able to forget…a taste I don't want to forget.

"He was the best part of life," I say to Mom.

She's calmed down now and is resting with her head in my lap. "I could tell that you two loved each other from the second you both walked in. Why don't you go be with him?" She sits up.

"Because as much as I want to do that, I want to be here with you more." I look at her, and tears return to her eyes.

"You are such a beautiful person, Penelope, inside and out." She hugs me tightly.

We hold each other and cry.

CHAPTER THIRTY

"I can't believe this is your last shift," Amelia says to me in the back kitchen of Coral's Café.

"It's time for me to move on. I am swamped with art orders."

I've received so many emails and custom-art requests that it's time for me to focus solely on my art. Mike, my manager, was bummed to hear I was quitting—not to mention Amelia who thinks it's the worst thing in the world.

"Do you promise that we will still see each other?" She gives me puppy eyes.

"Amelia, I see more of you outside of work than here. Aren't we going out tonight?" I ask, grabbing the French fries my table ordered.

I admire her love for me. It's been two weeks since Myles left, and I've been a mess. I broke down to her yesterday on our lunch break and told her how much I cared about him. She knew we had a thing for each other, just by the way he looked at me, but didn't know there was deep *love* involved.

"Yes, we are going out tonight. You need to look hot so you can get some male attention and get your mind off of Myles," she says, winking.

She invited me to a bonfire beach party. I'm actually looking forward to going; I need to get out of my apartment. I've only left it to visit my mom and to go to work. My bed has been the only place I find solace. I feel disgusted to admit that I haven't washed the sheets, for fear that doing so will rid them of Myles's lingering scent. I wear his hoodie every day to work, and I wear it every night to sleep. *To say I am pathetic is an understatement.*

I ignored Amelia's request to look hot and showed up at the beach meeting place in the same hoodie and shorts. I don't want male attention, and I certainly don't want to get my mind off Myles. Even though I can't be with him physically, I can still hold on to him emotionally.

I look around and don't recognize anyone but Amelia. She waves me over to come sit with her near the fire.

"Here, take this." She hands me a drink.

I take a sip—rum and pineapple juice.

"I thought we agreed to dress up a bit," she says, wide-eyed at my outfit.

"WE didn't agree. YOU said to look hot. I just didn't listen."

"Fine, you get a pass tonight."

I sit there and listen to a couple of girls talk about these new guys they are dating, and I can't help but feel a tinge of regret.

I miss him so much. If he were here, I wouldn't be sitting around this fire, listening to the tales of random women and their flings. I'd be at home with Myles, nuzzled up on the sofa, watching a movie or, better yet, lying in bed with him. Agreeing to cut it off now, before it got deeper, seemed like a good idea, except it has already been deep for years.

I mindlessly listen to the girls and smile when I am supposed to. I came here to take my mind off things, and yet Myles is all that's on it.

"Is that Ben?" Amelia asks, pointing to the next fire over.

Ben and a girl are cozied up, sitting in front of their own personal fire. Her hand rests on his knee, and she has one leg flung over his. She's a slim brunette with the prettiest smile.

"Let's go say hi." Amelia stands up.

"Amelia, wait," I say, trying to stop her, but she's already walking over there. I excuse myself and quickly follow her.

"Hi, Ben," she says, standing in front of him and this girl.

"Oh hey, guys." He looks at me and stands up; the girl stands too. "This is Sophia." He puts his arm around her waist; she extends her hand for a handshake.

I return her gesture. "Sophia, it's really nice to meet you. I'm Penny," I say almost too happily.

He got her. He got Sophia back, and if that's not enough to make me want to break down again right here and right now, I don't know what is. I look at him and smile, sending a silent message that I am rooting for them.

He nods at me and smiles back.

When Ben used to speak about Sophia, his whole-body language changed. I think, when humans give their heart to another, there is a shift of energy, and I can see that in Ben right now. He's in heaven, and the woman standing next to him is his angel.

"So how does everyone know each other?" Sophia asks, retaking her seat.

"From work," I blurt. Amelia is unaware of Ben's love for Sophia, and I don't want her to say anything inappropriate, so I do my best to intervene.

Confused, Amelia glances at me. "Yeah, at work," she confirms. "How about the two of you?" Amelia pries.

"We met in college," Sophia says, grinning at Ben.

He smiles back at her and shakes his head in agreement.

"Well, we just wanted to come by and say hi. You two enjoy your night," I say and grab Amelia's arm.

"Why are you being so weird?" she whispers as we walk away.

"Sophia is Ben's lover from college. He used to talk about her and how much he missed her. I didn't want the conversation to go anywhere that would ruin that," I say sternly.

"Got it," she says, plopping back onto the sand. "I'll admit they look really happy," she comments.

I glance back over and see Sophia laying her head on Ben's shoulder and laughing. No engagement ring in sight.

At least he got his happy ending.

I stay with Amelia for another hour or so and then head home. I told her I just needed some sleep. She didn't ask many questions, but I'm sure she could tell I was over it.

Lying in bed, I pull out my phone and open Myles's contact. I stare at his name and stop myself from calling him.

I wonder if he's ever done the same.

Chapter Thirty-One

Five Months Later

"Mom, you really need to drink this," I say to her while handing her a cup of freshly pressed juice. "It's full of all kinds of nutrients."

"Penny, I really don't want to; it smells funny." She makes an *"ick"* face.

"Please, just drink it for me," I say, nudging it towards her again.

"Ugh, okay, fine." She takes it and chugs it as quickly as she can.

She was diagnosed with coronary artery disease five months ago, just right after Myles left. It's been a rough time since then, and her health has declined quite a bit.

It took me forever to accept Myles's leaving. There were countless times I almost pressed Call on his name in my phone. It was especially hard when Mom received her diagnosis, but the doctors are optimistic; as long as she takes her medication, there shouldn't be any issues.

I've been researching all kinds of natural fruits and vegetables that are good for heart health, and have been bringing her fresh pressed juices daily. It's part of my daily routine—see Mom, work on my art—plus a weekly get-together with Amelia. She's been connected at the hip with Scott this entire time. I'm certain she's in love with him, and I can confidently say that they are one the most smitten couples I have ever seen.

"Penny, I'm going to be fine," Mom says.

"I know, but this stuff can't hurt." It's weird seeing Mom so exhausted. Some days are better than others. "Let's go for a little walk and get some fresh air."

She nods and stands up.

The path behind the center is gorgeous. It's surrounded by palm trees, shrubbery, and all kinds of flowers. It has taken me back to the days in Coupeville multiple times, and I think it does the same for my mom. She's always happier when we are outside.

So am I.

"How is business?" she asks, touching the tip of a white daisy.

"It's great! I have all kinds of pieces to finish and send out this week."

She always asks about my art; she likes to see pictures of what I have completed and what I'm working on. Sometimes I bring them in and let her add her own personal touch to make that piece just a little more special.

I'm content with life at the moment. A hole inside of me will always be present as long as Myles isn't with me, but being here with my mom means everything. We've had multiple conversations about my childhood, the good and the bad. We have been able to tackle one topic at a time and stop if it becomes too much for either of us.

I finally sold the house in Port Townsend too. I just stashed away the money in a savings account. I offered to give it to my mother, but she insisted I keep it. She said she has no use for money. Instead, we occasionally go out and splurge here and there. Otis and I take her out a few times a month. We'll go shopping and get lunch. I try to recreate what I think a normal mother/daughter relationship should be, and for the most part, it is.

"Look at these roses." She gestures towards a bush full of deep-red roses. "I know they are very common, but I still feel they are underrated," she says, admiring their beauty.

"Just like us," I joke.

She giggles. "The breeze is nice," she says, closing her eyes and letting her face bask in the small gleam of sunlight that is peeking through the clouds. I watch her stand there, so grateful for that little bit of sunshine.

"Let's head back, honey. I need to lie down." She starts to walk back towards the building.

"Okay, no problem, Mom," I say and link my arm with hers.

We head back to her room; she lies down on the bed and cuddles up with a pillow. "Thank you for taking care of me, baby," she says, trying to keep her eyes open.

"Of course, I love you, Mom," I say while tucking her in.

"I love you too." She smiles tiredly and shuts her eyes.

I watch her drift into a sweet slumber and let myself out quietly. I run into Otis as I'm leaving.

"How is she?" he asks.

"She's tired. We went on a walk, but it didn't last very long."

"She's going to be okay, Penny. The medications are keeping everything normal; exhaustion is a very common side effect." He places his hand on my shoulder and offers a look of reassurance.

"I know. Thanks, Otis. I'll come by tomorrow."

"See you then," he says and quietly opens Mom's door to set a cup of pills on her nightstand.

I adore seeing how much Otis loves and cares for my mother. He even made her a homemade coconut cake for her last birthday, which he doesn't do for all his patients.

It's almost Christmas, so the center is covered in miniature Christmas trees, ornaments, and tinsel. They play soft Christmas music in the common areas too, which I secretly love. Grandpa never played Christmas music growing up, nor did he ever decorate. I don't either. I don't see the point when I am the only one at home, but I do enjoy the decorations in the places around me.

Amelia and her family invited me to their Christmas dinner again this year, but I politely declined and told them I'd be spending it at the recovery center with my mom. The residents are having a potluck dinner, so I offered to help Mom make a cherry pie.

I make my way to my Bronco; I have plenty of work to complete and need to get a head start. But before I am back in my car, a nurse comes running out.

"Penny! Come quick!" The urgency in her voice scares me.

I immediately turn around and run back into the center. I see nurses and doctors flocking to my mom's room. She's on the floor, and they are performing CPR.

"What's happening?" I demand.

Otis comes over to me. "She had a heart attack. We woke her up to take her pills, and she just fell to the floor," he says to me slowly.

"How? I just saw her." I start to panic. "She was okay; she was just tired." I frantically try to make sense of all of this.

They continue to do CPR.

"Otis, talk to me!" I yell.

He tries to calm me down, but I push him away and attempt to get closer to my mom. Another male nurse comes over and keeps me in position.

"Let me go! Let me see her!" I scream and try to claw my way out of his grasp.

"Penny, you need to calm down." Otis is in front of me now, but he's just a blur.

I zone out, and everything is quiet; ringing floods my ears. I stand still and mindlessly watch the nurses carry my mother's body out on a stretcher. Everything is in slow motion.

I can feel Otis pulling me into a hug, but my arms won't move to return his embrace. "Penny...Penny..." I keep hearing him say, but I can't take my eyes off Mom.

She's dead, and I wish I were too.

CHAPTER THIRTY-TWO

The funeral was a small gathering at a cemetery that sat on top of a cliff, overlooking the ocean. Otis and some other of the recovery staff were there. Amelia and her parents came for support as well.

I had always thought cremation was the way to go, but Otis told me that my mom asked to be buried if she were to die in his care. She wanted to be a part of the earth again, worms and all. Reincarnation was something she talked about often. She once told me that this was her fourth life on this planet and that she would reincarnate as a giant Douglas fir tree in her next one.

The center sent a beautiful flower arrangement to the funeral; my mom would have loved it. I bet she could name every flower and paint them all perfectly. They gave it to me to take home and told me if I needed anything to reach out.

"We have taken care of everything," Otis says as he walks me to my car; Amelia follows a few feet behind.

"Thank you, Otis."

"Please reach out if you need anything. You shouldn't be alone right now," he says sadly. I know he misses her just as much as I do.

"I will. I hope you have a nice Christmas," I say to him and hug him goodbye.

It's Christmas Eve and any amount of joy I had for this holiday has disappeared, but I am grateful for the people who chose to spend some of their holiday here at this dreary funeral. It's gloomy, and it has been sprinkling all morning, a perfect day for burying a body.

"Do you want me to come home with you?" Amelia asks, opening my car door.

"No, I'll be okay. Go spend the holiday with your family."

She holds me tightly for a minute. "I love you, Penny. I know you've heard this a million times, but everything will be okay." She offers a slight smile.

"Thank you, Amelia. I love you too."

She squeezes me in a tight hug and leaves.

I get into my Bronco and turn it on. I sit and stare as the rain starts to pour against the windshield. I turn the stereo up a little and let out an enormous scream. I let my head fall against my steering wheel, and I cry.

A familiar feeling rushes over me, and I remember sitting in my car right before I left Port Townsend. The pain I felt then matches what I feel now.

What did I do in my past life to deserve all of this?

I watch Leslie and Finn walk hand in hand to their vehicle. I see Otis wiping tears from his face, and I see the last bit of dirt thrown onto my mother's grave.

I try to calm down and allow myself to drive home. I walk into my apartment and drop my keys on the counter. My coat and hair are soaking wet, and mascara runs down my face.

"FUCK!" I scream out. *"WHY!"*

I grab one of the dining room chairs and throw it across the living room; one of the legs breaks off as it smashes to the floor. I stare out the window and watch the raindrops fall.

I could jump out of this window, but it's not high enough. I could drive my car into a wall, but I'd hate to leave that mess for someone to clean up.

I hate everything. The art on my wall, the color of the couch, the various plants that line my patio. None of it matters anymore.

There is only one way I know how to escape this torture, and it's to leave it all behind.

Otis dropped off her clothes, jewelry, and artwork a couple of days later. He also brought me some groceries, assuming I hadn't eaten much. He was right. I haven't eaten or slept since my mother died.

Amelia was kind enough to notify all my current customers and let them know there would be a delay in delivering their pieces. She's been great and has checked in on me every day. I'm usually in the same spot when she comes over—in bed, pretending to be asleep. She told me I need to reach out to a therapist for extra support and grieving tools.

A therapist may be able to help, but I don't have the energy to interview any of them. I don't really want to talk about what happened. My mother is gone again, this time permanently.

I need time.

I feel as if I'm seventeen again, throwing all of my belongings into paint-stained duffel bags. Gathering my art and supplies and shoving them into the back of my Bronco. Amelia will just have to understand; I can't call her. She'll try to stop me, and with the sisterly love I have for her, she may succeed.

I can't be in this place anymore; there is nothing left for me. I've come full circle with the last traumatic event I encountered, and I'm running away…again.

I rev the engine of my Bronco and screech off. I pass the street where Coral's Café sits. I pass the beach where Myles and I shared loving moments. I pass the recovery center, and my heart tears open.

I've cried a lot in my life, but never as much as now. Once again, the woman whom I loved with my entire being is gone. But this time it is definite that I will never see her again.

I didn't even say goodbye.

I drive and drive and only stop for gas. I don't need food; I don't need sleep. I just need to get to where I'm going to bring some sort of contentment to my broken world.

CHAPTER THIRTY-THREE

Twenty-two very long hours later, I park in front of a little blue house in Coupeville, Washington. I've been sitting here for ten minutes, hiding the best I can behind a big tree.

The house has clearly been sold, and someone appears to be living in it. There is a red truck in the driveway, the grass is luscious and freshly mowed, and it looks warmer than ever before. I notice some of the vines have been trimmed back too; they look livelier than ever.

I came here to bury my mother's things in her old flower garden in the backyard. I thought it would be fitting. I don't have a plan of where to go next; maybe I'll live in my car again and travel until I find a place where no harm can reach me. *I wonder if a place like that even exists anywhere.*

I have a newfound hatred for San Diego, and the only place I could think of that may offer some kind of temporary comfort was the home I used to live in. Memories of wonderful times with my mom haunt me as I sit and stare at my old house, but it's better than remembering her lifeless face. I replay the image of her lying dead on a stretcher in my mind. I shudder at the memory.

I gather the courage to get out of the Bronco and attempt to explain to the homeowner why I'm here. I grab the bag of my mom's things and head to the door.

Knock, knock, knock.

A beautiful man opens the door, and I see my painting —the blue Chevy truck with a white stripe, parked in front of a starlit forest—hanging over the fireplace. The man has sandy-blond hair and bright-blue eyes.

For a minute, I wonder if I'm in heaven. *Maybe I'm dead, and the angel in front of me is welcoming me into the heavenly bliss of a new forever home.* I'm okay with that outcome. My heaven would be right here in this house with *him.*

I suddenly drop the bag, and everything I have been holding inside my body comes rushing out as he pulls me into his arms.

"I've got you, baby." He holds me tightly and presses his head to mine.

I let every painful memory seep out of me and dissipate as I stand in my tear-soaked clothes and embrace him. "What are you doing here?" I ask between sobs, allowing myself to completely let every guard down.

"I've been waiting for you," he says, smiling his perfect smile.

I remember his words— *"The next time we are together, I'm not leaving, and I'm not letting you go."*

I think, for the first time ever, I am finally where I am supposed to be.

Chapter Thirty-Four

Myles

She thinks she's cursed, broken even. I think she's a blessing, and she makes me whole. She told me once that we don't understand the reasons things happen until later in life, and she was right.

I tried to find her when I learned she had left Port Townsend, but she was nowhere to be found. She was a ghost. I even tried to get it out of her awful grandfather, but he knew nothing. I kept looking, day in and day out, trying to find some sort of inkling of her whereabouts.

I finally stumbled across her art page. I knew she was going to be in Seattle. I knew she'd be at the wedding, and there wasn't a chance in hell that I was going to miss that.

That morning, I tried to find her at the art convention, but she wasn't there. I caught a glimpse of a solitary piece of art on the wall, the painting she had done of my

Chevy truck. All this time, she had to have been thinking of me as much as I was thinking of her.

Seeing her at Whalen and Lacey's wedding was surreal. I remember her standing there in her long, silky yellow dress, her hair down to her lower back. All I could mutter was her name; "Penelope Wolfe" rolled off my tongue way too easily.

When she turned, I noticed she still wore the necklace I gave her, and that told me all that I needed to know. She still loved me…in some manner at least.

Kissing her that night had me lost in a world of serenity. Leaving her that night was equivalent to ripping my own heart out.

Once I'd found her, I had every intention of following her. But after some research, I discovered how hard it would be to transfer from Seattle to Pacific Beach. If I left Seattle, it would mean starting my career over and leaving everything I had worked for in the dust.

So I bought her old house in Coupeville and transferred there instead. Just in case she one day came back to me. I knew how much she loved this home; she talked about it constantly and recreated it in her art pieces. If she wasn't the one living there, I would be the placeholder until she was. The painting sits perfectly above the fireplace, and it brings me back to her every time I look at it.

When I saw she was holding her own art show, I figured it would be the perfect time to profess my undying love to her. To whisk her away, back to our home state, to live out our lives together. Instead, I learned she had been reunited with her mother, whom she needed more than anyone, including me. What kind of man would I be to make her choose between us?

I settled for taking in every second I could get of her. When we said goodbye in San Diego, I wholeheartedly believed that I would never see her again. That was our plan, anyway, until the universe intervened.

I can see why Penny loved this house; it has so much character. Even more so, it is a symbol of her. Strong but delicate, adorned with beauty and grace in every corner. I can imagine her sitting in the backyard with an easel, some paint, and a flower in her hair.

When I opened the door and saw her beautiful green, tear-filled eyes, I knew it was finally our time.

Now, she rests in my arms, in *our* home, after a long day of planting some new Douglas firs. She didn't tell me why she insisted on those, but I know, for whatever the reason, it is important.

I'll repay the cosmos by nurturing her as if she were a priceless piece of treasure. She is, of course, nothing less than that to me.

Let's Connect

Find out more about Rose D. Bentley
at the following links!

Official Website: www.rosedbentley.com

Facebook: Rose D. Bentley

Tik-tok: @rosiebee12312

Instagram: @rosedbentley

Printed in the USA
CPSIA information can be obtained
at www.ICGtesting.com
LVHW041046290923
758980LV00004B/20